HUNTER SECURITY BOOK TWO

LAURA JOHN

Independently published.

Cover Designer: Brittany Franks with Chaotic Creatives

Editor: Swish Design and Editing

Sensitivity Reader: J.P Jackson

Mandy and Michelle if I ever decide to be a stripper I'm letting you choose my name!

Dear Reader,

This book touches on a few sensitive and heavy subjects that could be difficult for some to read.

If you think there is a subject that could be a problem for you, please proceed to my website for a complete list of content warnings.

https://www.authorlaurajohn.com/denver

Author Note

This book has some medical scenes that have been glazed over slightly and some timelines have been sped up to keep the pace of the story. While i try to keep things as accurate as possible this is a romance book and it's sometimes not possible to go into all the details and keep the story moving. Also every person heals differntly and I did a lot of research to keep it as close to reality as possible.

Prologue

FORD

Seven and a half months ago

I FUCKING HATE MORNINGS.

Thankfully, I'm next in line to order my drink from the best coffee shop in town.

"Hey, Ford." A voice belonging to a person I'll never be able to forget pulls my attention from the front counter.

I turn to find Samantha, my ex-girlfriend, standing there looking effortlessly amazing. Her ginger hair is piled high in her usual messy bun, with a few wispy strands escaping. Her makeup is subtle, highlighting her natural beauty, just the way I've always liked it. A shy smile is on her plump lips, covered in a sheer gloss.

I bet it tastes like raspberries. It's her favorite flavor. And I should know—we were together for almost a decade.

I almost hate that she looks so good right now.

"Hey, Samantha, it's been a while," I reply right before the barista calls me forward.

I'm thankful for the conversation break, but this tingling in the base of my spine tells me this isn't a coincidence. Being in the line of work I am, as a police officer and now detective for almost twenty years, has taught me to trust my gut instincts.

"I've been trying to reach out, but I understand why you haven't been returning my calls," she says once I've ordered my coffee, moving to another line to wait.

See? Not happenstance. She's tracked me down. But why? She was the one who broke up with me and forced me to move in with my best friend.

"Work's been busy," I half lie.

Work *has* been crazy, but it's not the reason I've been avoiding her calls.

"Well, thankfully, your habits never change, and I was able to find you here..." She pauses, pressing her lips together. She glances at the floor as she shifts from one foot to the other. "Could we talk for a minute?" she requests, but before I can respond, she holds her hand up and sighs. "Don't try telling me you have to get to work. We both know you have over an hour before your shift starts."

I blow out a breath and run a hand through my short hair. My nails scrape against my scalp in a way that grounds me.

"Okay," I tell her as my name is called.

After grabbing my coffee, I follow her to a table in the corner of the café.

"What's up?" I ask as we take our seats.

"I'm not sure how to tell you this," she murmurs.

I wonder what bombshell she's about to drop on me. What could she possibly need to tell me that would warrant tracking me down like this? Maybe she's found her perfect match and is getting married and doesn't want me to find out from someone else.

It's only been two months since we broke up, but I've been told women emotionally break up with men long before they physically do it. Maybe she found someone who wants the same things in life she does.

Apparently, that guy wasn't me.

"It's usually best just to spit it out," I encourage her, wanting to get this conversation over with.

She closes her eyes and takes a deep inhale through her nose, then exhales through her mouth. Once her gorgeous green eyes open again, she says words I never thought I'd hear.

"I'm pregnant."

My chest becomes so fucking tight I struggle to breathe. "What?" I question, gasping for air.

A little giggle escapes her lips, and she brushes a lock of hair that fell from her bun out of her face. "I had a similar reaction when I read the test before I broke down in tears, of course."

I open my mouth to respond but close it as my mind goes completely blank.

Samantha doesn't want kids. It's one of the reasons we broke up. I wanted to settle down and have a family, but she didn't. When she pictured the rest of her life, kids were *not* a part of that, and I couldn't see a life *without* them.

"What do you want to do?" I ask once my brain comes back online.

Her smile is warm as she reaches across the table and rests her hand on top of mine. "I've asked myself that same question a million times since I found out," she tells me. "I still don't want kids... but I know you do, and taking that away from you without talking with you first doesn't feel right."

"What are you saying?"

"If you want to be a dad, I'll carry the baby for you. You can be a single dad until you find the right woman for you. I'm already pregnant, so I thought, why not offer this to you? I know I broke your heart when I called things off, and I'm so sorry."

Her words are quiet, but they make a big impact.

I flip my hand to give hers a squeeze. "Why don't we do this together?" I request, but she shakes her head.

"I'd resent the baby and you. I don't want that. If you don't want to be a single dad, I understand, but I won't be keeping the baby. I'll probably have an abortion. I meant what I said when we broke up. Kids aren't something I want in my life."

I mull over her words for a minute, trying to come up with a response. "So you'd pretty much be a surrogate, for lack of a better term?"

She nods with a small smile. "This is your child, Ford. If you want it, I'll do this for you. I love you, but we just weren't meant for each other. Once the baby's born, I'm gone. I'm actually planning on moving to Miami."

"You got the job?" I ask.

Her face lights up with pure joy, and she says, "Yes."

Samantha has been wanting to work for the world's hottest fashion company for almost as long as we were together. She is an amazing designer, and they'll be lucky to have her.

"I did, but I have up to a year to move. I'll be working remotely until then."

"I'm so happy for you, Samantha. I'm sorry I held you back for so long."

She shakes her head and squeezes my hand. "You didn't hold me back. I did that to myself, and in a way, I held *you* back. I was hoping I would change how I felt about kids, but it never happened. I should have broken up with you sooner. I'm the one who's sorry."

I'll always love Samantha, and I think she'll always love me too, but like she said, we weren't meant to be together.

"Can I take a day or two before I give you an answer?" I ask.

"Of course. I know it's a shock. Just let me know as soon as you can."

I nod and stand up. Samantha does the same and pulls me into her arms for a hug.

"Take care, Ford," she whispers, then walks out of the coffee shop ahead of me.

"YOU LOOK LIKE SHIT," Denver, my best friend and now roommate, notes when I walk through the door.

When Samantha and I broke up, we agreed it would be best for her to keep the house and for me to move out. Seeing as the housing market is so expensive right now, Denver suggested I move in with him, and I've been here ever since.

I was planning on buying my own place one day, but with a baby on the way, I might have to do that sooner rather than later.

My feet carry me further into the house, and the aroma of what Denver is cooking almost makes things better.

"I ran into Samantha this morning. It made for a long day at work," I murmur as I play through our conversation for the millionth time today.

His gray eyes are wide as he sucks in air. "Damn... what did she have to say?"

"She's pregnant," I blurt out, and Denver almost drops the plate he's holding.

"Really? So are you getting back together?" he asks with a look of confusion, and something that almost comes across as hurt appears on his face.

Why would he be upset by the idea of Samantha and me getting back together? Maybe he just doesn't want me to get hurt again.

Thoughts of the night Samantha and I broke up flutter into my head, and my chest aches again. There was so much yelling that night, and when I showed up on Denver's doorstep, initially just for a night or two, my eyes were swollen from how much I had cried. I didn't want to give up on the relationship, but there was no saving it. For a solid two weeks, I stayed holed up in my bedroom, only leaving to go to work. Denver finally had enough and forced me to come out of hiding. He's the reason I started smiling again.

I shake my head. "She still doesn't want kids, but she offered to have the baby if I wanted it, but I'd be a single dad. I'm not sure how I'd raise a kid on my own, but saying no to this opportunity feels wrong too."

"You wouldn't be alone," Denver replies matter-of-factly.

I stare at him like he grew a second head. "What do you mean? Did you miss the part where Samantha doesn't want this? She'll be moving to Miami as soon as the baby is born. I'll need to find a new place to live, figure out childcare, plan a million things, and it's terrifying."

Denver lets out a low chuckle, which makes my blood boil, and I glare at him.

"You're a little dense sometimes," he mutters.

I can't think of a response, so I stare him down instead.

"You have *me*, dumbass," he states after an awkward staring contest. "I'd never let you do this on your own. You've always wanted kids, Ford, since we were kids ourselves. You can't give this up. Accept her offer, get a good lawyer to make sure everything is fair, and have this baby. We'll figure everything else out after."

Tears prickle behind my eyes as I walk up to him and wrap my arms around him for a tight hug. Denver's spine briefly goes stick straight before he relaxes and returns my hug.

"Thanks for being the best," I whisper, patting his back before stepping away.

"It's what friends are for," he responds, running his hands over his jeans. He looks nervous, but I have no idea why. "How 'bout we eat and discuss what we are going to do. Remember, you're not alone in this."

I take a deep breath as he sets our plates on the table.

How did I get so lucky to get a friend like this?

Chapter One

DENVER

Present day

"HEY, SAMANTHA," I ANSWER my phone, leaning back in my office chair. "What's up?"

"Ford won't answer his phone, and I'm on my way to the hospital. The baby's coming. He can't miss this," she whimpers and then screams.

"Oh my God. Are you okay?"

"Another contraction. These are fucking horrible. The second this baby is out, I'm getting my tubes tied," she grumbles.

I almost laugh, but there is a strong possibility that would piss her off. "I'll find Ford and get him to the hospital," I assure her before she yells again.

"Hurry. I'm not sure how long until this baby will be here."

I hit end, select Ford's name, and press the call button.

"Fuck," I mutter under my breath when it goes to voicemail.

Thankfully, I have the station's number programmed into my phone and call there next.

"It's Denver. I'm looking for Detective Daniels," I say after Meredith answers the call.

"He stepped out for lunch a few minutes ago. Can I take a message?" she asks.

"If he returns before I find him, tell him to call Denver. It's an emergency," I say, then end the call.

Rushing out of my office, I tell our secretary I'll be gone for the afternoon, then race to my car. I pray to God Ford went to his normal place for lunch and didn't randomly choose somewhere new.

The bell on the door of Ford's favorite diner rings loudly as I fling it open. I instantly blow out a breath of relief when my eyes land on him.

His back is to me, and he's reading a book. *What a nerd.* Yet the image turns me on. I'm not sure how that's hot, but it seems like everything Ford does turns me on ever since I figured out I'm not as straight as I once thought. But this isn't the time to contemplate whatever this is.

"We've got to go," I tell him when I arrive at his table.

"What are you doing here?" he almost squeaks out, his ocean eyes wide.

"Samantha's in labor. We both tried calling you, but our calls kept going to voicemail."

"Shit," he murmurs, pulling his phone out from his pocket. "I turned it on silent when I was interviewing someone earlier. I forgot to turn the ringer back on. I'm so sorry."

His brows are pulled together, and he shakes his head. I hate how upset with himself he looks right now.

"It happens," I console him. "But we have to go. Your baby is about to be born."

His sandy-blond brows shoot up at the reminder, and he bolts up, throwing a twenty on the table to cover the cost of the lunch he didn't get to eat.

"I'm having a baby," he whispers, his voice laced with anxious energy as he follows me outside.

"Where are you parked?" I search the area but don't see his car.

"I left it at the station. It's only a few blocks away, so I walked today."

"I'm parked this way," I tell him, tilting my head, our steps quickly covering the ground to my car.

"Are you sure we're ready for this?" he questions as we get in, moving to secure his gun in my glove box that, thanks to my job, has a decent lock for when I need to do the same.

"Ready as we'll ever be," I respond with a shrug, driving to the hospital as fast as possible.

When Ford came home almost eight months ago telling me Samantha was pregnant, I was shocked and jealous. I thought for sure they would be getting back together. I didn't think that a few minutes later I would be agreeing to help him raise a baby. But I know my best friend better than anyone else, and he's always wanted a family, so I couldn't say no, even if it meant burying my desires.

Now, I'll simply have to figure out how to keep my feelings at bay. I've done a pretty good job since they showed up almost a year ago.

The memory of that night floods my mind unsolicited.

Today has been a day from hell, and all I want is an ice-cold beer and maybe to hang out with Ford.

Fetching my phone from my pocket, I send off a text before heading to the kitchen.

Me: *Want to come over for a beer?*
Ford: *Can't. I need to spend time with Samantha.*

I shake my head, knowing how crazy their relationship has been since almost the beginning. They are constantly on and off again.

Me: *Good luck with that.*
Ford: *Thanks. I might be free this weekend.*
Me: *Sounds good.*

Since hanging out with my best friend is a bust, and there is no way I want to go out, I head to the living room and turn on a random show.

About halfway through the second episode, my phone buzzes on the coffee table. I reach forward and snicker, seeing that it's Ford.

Date night must not be going so well.

After I swipe open the message, I drop my phone in shock.

What the fuck!

My heart is racing a mile a minute, and my mouth is instantly dry.

Did I just see what I thought I saw?

With a shaky hand, I pick my phone up again and gasp.

Yup, that's a dick pic from my best friend.

Ford: *Waiting for you.*

It's obvious the message isn't meant for me. He must have hit my contact info by accident. I should delete it right away and tell Ford about the mistake, but that isn't what I do. Instead, I stare at the picture.

Ford's cock is impressive. It's not ridiculously thick, but it's long—easily two and a half fist lengths. My own dick grows as I take in the image in front of me.

What the fuck is happening to me?

Again, I drop my phone and then rub a hand over my face.

I've seen Ford naked when we shower at the gym together, and I've never once gotten hard from it. So why is this accidental picture turning me on?

Searching my brain, I try to figure out when I last got laid. Considering nothing is coming to mind, it's been far too long.

I pick up my phone, this time trying not to look at the picture, and instead pull up some good porn with a hot woman, praying it will get Ford's dick out of my mind.

Scrolling through my favorite website, none of the couples pique my interest, but I click on a random one anyway. Once the video starts, I pull my cock out and stroke it, but I struggle to stay hard. The woman's tits are bouncing as the man fucks her, and normally I'd be at least turned on by now, yet my dick keeps deflating.

"Fuck," I yell, exiting out of the video.

My phone buzzes at that moment, and sweat breaks across my brow as Ford's name pops up. Thankfully, I can see the beginning of the message and know it isn't another sext. But I do, unfortunately, have to see the picture again to read the entire thing.

Ford: *Shit, man! I'm so sorry. That was meant for Samantha, not you!*

Not wanting him to know how the picture affected me, I try to play it cool.

Me: *Figured as much. Not sure why she stays with you, though. That's a small cock.*

Ford: *Fuck you. I bet I'm bigger.*

Me: *Only in your dreams.*

Ford: *Shit, Samantha just got here. Got to go.*

Me: Hope she enjoys your tiny ride.
Ford: *Middle finger emoji**

If I weren't so confused right now, I'd be laughing, but instead, I'm freaking the fuck out.

I push myself off the couch, pacing and running my fingers through my hair.

What the fuck does this mean? How long have I felt like this? *But even as I question myself, my cock throbs at the image I won't soon forget. I release a deep breath, stopping myself from wearing a permanent path on the carpet.*

The weight of the image hangs heavy in my hand, and even though I shouldn't, I scroll up and stare at the picture on my screen again. My cock likes it a lot, and although my stomach is knotted with shame, I sit back down and stroke myself.

It doesn't take long to get fully hard, and suddenly, the thought of sucking his long dick pops into my head, and a fucked-up fantasy starts to take place. I pick up the pace of my stroking as my eyes flutter shut, and my imagination plays a scene of me choking on my best friend's cock.

And just like that, I blow my load all over my fist and stomach, and I'm left feeling empty in more ways than one.

Apparently, I'm not as straight as I thought I was, but what the fuck do I do with this information? It's not like I planned on having this weird awakening at thirty-seven years old. Maybe this is a one-time thing, *I think, lying to myself and deciding it has to be stress from work.*

It has to be.

A sign for the hospital exit pulls my attention back to the present, and I internally shake my head. It's not fucking smart to daydream while driving. *What if I had gotten us into an accident?*

"You okay?" Ford asks after I huff out a breath, and I nod.

"Yup. I'm fine," I respond, even though I'm anything *but* fine right now.

It's not like I can tell him the truth. It's been a year, and I still struggle with coming to terms with the fact that I'm bi. It's something I am constantly questioning, even as my attraction for my best friend grows.

I was able to bring up sexuality to my friends—who are also my coworkers and one is my boss—and according to them, it's a fluid thing. People find out things at different times in life, but it still takes time to wrap your head around. Maybe that's why I still haven't come out to anyone. Or maybe I'm still in a state of denial.

I'm sure they know something is up from how I acted after I received the picture, but they're letting me come to them on my terms, which I'm thankful for. There's no doubt in my mind that they'll be accepting. Most of them aren't straight either, so you'd think I'd want to open up more, but I'm not ready.

I'm more afraid of how other people in my life will take the news. Like my *straight* best friend, who I'm going to be helping raise a kid and also have a crush on. I'm *sure* he would love to find out I'm bi, and I can't lose him.

I'll simply have to keep a lid on this for a while longer. One day, he'll have a handle on being a single dad and won't need me anymore. After he moves out, I'll tell him. It will be safer that way.

"I'm looking for Samantha Burk," Ford tells a lady at the front desk, bringing me back to the present. "She's having my baby."

The lady smiles and gives us directions to labor and delivery.

" 'Bout time you showed up," Samantha yells when Ford and I enter the delivery room side by side.

Her face is red and sweaty, and her legs are in stirrups. I'm wondering if I should even be here.

"The baby is almost here, Dad," the doctor tells Ford, then looks at me. "You can wait in the room down the hall."

I nod, but as I turn to leave, Ford grips my forearm. "Stay, please," he begs.

Samantha rolls her eyes. "Denver can stay. He'll probably be more helpful than Ford anyway. He doesn't do well when I'm in pain."

The doctor shrugs and guides us to a spot out of the way.

"You've got this," Ford praises Samantha.

She glares at him. "I'm not sure why I agreed to this. It hurts so fucking bad."

"Did you get the epidural?" I ask.

Tears pool in Samantha's sapphire eyes. "The baby is impatient like its father and is coming too fast. I didn't have time to get the drugs," she whimpers out before screaming.

"That's it, Samantha, give me three big pushes," the doctor coaches. "Would you like to see the head, Dad?"

Ford's face is green as he shakes his head.

"Can I look?" I ask Samantha.

"Be my guest. I've already had a million people look at my hoo-ha today. What's one more?"

I press my lips together to stop the laugh as I peek at the head full of hair on Ford's baby.

"That's amazing," I whisper in awe.

When I turn my attention back to Ford, it's obvious he's trying to stay in the moment by taking deep breaths, but I'm seriously worried he's about to pass out.

"Sit in that chair," I instruct with a tilt of my head to the corner of the room. "I'll help Samantha."

He gulps, his Adam's apple bobbing with the motion, then moves to sit. *At least I don't have to worry about him anymore.*

"You've got this, Samantha," I remind her.

Her smile is bright in response, and she locks eyes with her doctor, a look of pure determination plastered on her face.

After that, the baby doesn't take long to arrive.

Ford is the first to hold the little boy. "I'm a dad," he murmurs with tears in his eyes.

"You look good holding him," Samantha whispers with pride beaming in her eyes.

"Would you like to hold him?" he asks.

She shakes her head. "He's yours, but I'm happy I could do this for you. Sorry for all the mean things I said while in labor."

Ford chuckles. "I deserved them. I'm sorry I wasn't more help."

"At least you have an amazing best friend." Samantha turns her attention to me and reaches to squeeze my hand. "Thank you."

I wave her off. "It was nothing. How are you doing?" I'm drawn to the fact that she's struggling to keep her eyes open.

"I'm feeling a little funny," she responds so quietly I almost don't hear her.

Her eyes flutter shut as loud beeping fills the room.

"What's going on?" Ford asks with a panic-laced tone.

I shake my head, trying to understand what is happening as a bunch of people fill the space.

"Let's take this sweet baby boy to the nursery," an older lady in scrubs with gray hair and kind eyes suggests while guiding Ford and me out of the room. Her name badge indicates she's a registered nurse, so I know it's best to do as she says.

"Is Samantha okay?" he asks, refusing to budge.

The nurse's smile fades a tiny bit before she responds. "She's in good hands."

Ford nods, but his eyes refuse to leave Samantha. It's almost as if he's in a daze as the lady takes his son and places him in the tiny plastic bassinet before wheeling him out of the room.

It's only when I grab his hand and give it a gentle tug that he finally looks away, and we follow the nurse down the hall.

It's been a long time since we were ushered out, and no one is giving us any answers. I won't lie and say I'm not scared.

Something feels wrong, but I can't put my finger on what it is.

"I'm getting pissed that they won't let us see Samantha," Ford grumbles, feeding his baby a bottle.

"I'm sure they will soon," I supply, but the words feel wrong. "Are you going to name him yet? Baby Daniels isn't the best," I tease.

"I'm not sure. I thought when I saw him, I would just know, but it's like there is a block in my brain."

I nod. "I guess that makes sense."

A knock on the door pulls our attention, and a pit fills my stomach when I notice Samantha's mother in the doorway. I didn't know she was here. She must have arrived sometime after we were moved into the nursery.

Her face is stained with tears, and I have a feeling what she's about to tell us isn't good news.

"No..." Ford whispers, holding his son closer.

Tears trickle down his face, and I know his stupid brain is playing out his worst fears as he clutches his son like a lifeline.

"She's alive," Mary whimpers out, and I let out a breath of relief I wasn't aware I was holding. "But there were complications. She'll never be able to have more children."

Ford gasps, and he shakes his head. "I know she didn't want to be a mother, but now that choice has been taken away from her. I never should have asked her to do this."

I rush to his side to offer him any comfort I can.

"You didn't ask her, she offered," Mary reminds him. "Samantha needs to rest, but in the morning, you should talk to her. I just thought it would be best for you to get the news from someone you know. It was scary for a bit there, and I thought we were going to lose her, but she's alive. We have to be thankful for that."

He nods and tries to take deep breaths. I gingerly take the beautiful little boy from his arms, and Ford thanks me with a nod, then stands to give Mary a hug.

"I'm so grateful she's still alive," he mutters into her neck.

"Me too."

Tears of my own sting my eyes as I glance down at the sleeping angel.

"You should name him Sammy," I say. "Samantha is a fighter, and being named after someone like that will make a strong little boy."

Ford's tear-filled eyes light up the smallest amount at my sugges-tion. "It's perfect," he tells me.

"I like it too," Mary says. "I've been meaning to ask, but I didn't know when the right time would be. Would you mind if I visited him from time to time?"

"I'd love that," Ford tells her, the corners of his lips turning up. "Regardless of Samantha's choice, you're always Sammy's grandma. The more people who love him, the better."

"Would you like to hold him?" I offer, trying to bring the moment back to something of joy.

Mary beams at me. "I'd love that," she responds, and I gently pass Sammy to her.

She coos at him, whispering words of love and adoration to the little boy, but I keep my attention on Ford, who appears to be spiraling.

"You good?" I ask as I stand near him, keeping my voice low.

He tilts his head but doesn't respond.

"I need to get back to Samantha, but thank you for this moment," Mary tells us, setting Sammy in my arms again.

She gives Ford another hug, tells us goodbye, and leaves to be with her daughter.

"Thank you for being here," Ford says after she's gone.

"That's what best friends are for," I remind him.

I carefully set Sammy down in his bassinet before wrapping my arms around my best friend.

It's obvious Ford is feeling guilty that Samantha can't have more kids. That's the kind of guy he is. It's going to take him a while to get through this, but thankfully, Samantha is still alive. The loss of her would have destroyed him.

I know they aren't together anymore, but part of him will always love her, and now he has a son to raise, thanks to her kindness. There's no breaking the bond they share, and I could never be jealous of that. Samantha is an amazing woman. She simply wasn't made to be Ford's forever partner.

While Ford deals with everything, he's going to need me even more. I hope to be the strength he needs while fighting this secret inside me.

Chapter Two

FORD

"He's so handsome," Samantha says, reaching out to stroke the side of Sammy's face. "I still can't believe you named him after me."

"Well, you're a strong, badass woman. We wanted that energy to rub off on this little man."

She giggles, then winces a little.

"Are you in pain?" I ask.

She rolls her eyes. "A little, but nothing like pushing out that crotch watermelon you're holding," she jokes.

I can't help but laugh. *God, that feels nice.* "I thought you were going to die," I admit quietly.

Samantha's hand moves to squeeze mine. "I was so out of it, so I'm not sure what I was thinking while it was all going down, but Mom said it was scary."

"I'm sorry you can't have more kids. I know babies weren't a part of your life plan, but it sucks that the choice has been taken away from you. I keep wanting to blame myself for that. This constant train of thought keeps running through my head, telling me if I wasn't selfish, none of this would have happened."

"I wanted to do this, Ford. You didn't pressure me into having Sammy. I knew the risks going into this. I made the decision on my own before coming to you. And I'd make the same one over and over again to witness the way your eyes sparkle when you look at that handsome little face."

The corners of my lips turn up at her response, easing some of the guilt inside me. "Have you changed your mind about wanting to be in his life?" I ask, and she shakes her head.

"Nope. I'd like to visit and give gifts from time to time, but I'm no mommy. I'll be like a kick-ass aunt he sees once in a while," she responds with a gorgeous yet tired grin.

"You should probably get more sleep. Denver will be back soon with the car seat and baby bag we forgot yesterday as we rushed to get here. When Sammy's discharged, we'll stop in to say goodbye."

"Sounds good. Thanks for checking on me."

"It's what friends are for," I remark and then head to the nursery with my son.

"READY TO GO?" DENVER asks with a big grin.

I blow out a breath as I clip the chest piece of Sammy's car seat harness and pull the tail to tighten the straps into place before double-checking that everything is correct and secure.

I move my head up and down to indicate I'm ready, but an anxious bubble fills my stomach. I'm excited to be bringing this little boy home, but I'm nervous I'm going to fuck it all up.

I don't normally get distressed like this. I'm a calm, cool, and collected kind of guy. When it comes to my job, and most of my life, I know what I need to do, and I get it done. My gut instincts are always right on the money and guide me in everything I do in life. But right now, it's like that intuition is out the window, and I'm floundering.

What the hell do I know about being a father?

A single dad to boot.

But there is no time to have second thoughts now. Sammy is here, and Samantha almost died bringing him into the world. It's time to man the fuck up and be the best dad I can be.

"I'll take him to say goodbye to Samantha," Denver offers, picking up my son in his car seat. "You have a few more forms to fill out."

I'm thankful as fuck to have my best friend by my side. At least I know if I fall, he'll be there to pick me up and give me the kick in the pants I'll need.

What would I do without him?

As I fill out the remaining paperwork, Denver returns, gently swaying a sleeping Sammy in the car seat. The nurse explains each page, and it all sinks in. I'm a dad taking my son home. My chest tightens, and I have to take a steadying breath at the realization.

When I glance at Denver, his focus is on my son, and again, I'm so damn grateful for him.

"That's it. Shall we head home?" I ask, gesturing to the door.

"Let's do this. I'll drive so you can sit in the back with Sammy."

I'm glad he made the suggestion because I hadn't even thought of that, but being apart from Sammy, even separated by only a row of seats, feels wrong right now.

After we get the car seat snapped into place, Denver drives us home while I fawn over my son, watching him sleep. Staring at him, I can't help but feel blessed.

My gaze shifts to Denver, and I catch him staring at me in the rearview mirror with a soft smile. "Thank you. I don't know what I'd do without you."

"Seriously, what are friends for?" he remarks, pulling into the driveway.

I'm beyond exhausted when we walk through the door to the house.

Maybe I should pass out when Sammy goes down.

"Are you hungry?" Denver asks, pulling me from my thoughts of sleep.

"I guess I could eat?" I respond as Sammy cries. "Seems like Little Man is hungry too."

"You give him a bottle, and I'll make lunch," Denver offers, and with my exhaustion, I'm appreciative.

"I'm glad you insisted on setting up the baby stuff early," I say, pulling Sammy out of his car seat and laying him down in the playpen in the living room.

The open floor plan of Denver's house allows me to keep an eye on Sammy while I warm up the bottle. He doesn't stop crying while I get his food ready, and my anxiety rises a bit. I know he's fine, and I have to get this bottle ready to satisfy his needs, but his whimpers are pulling at my heartstrings.

"Little Dude has a set of lungs on him," Denver notes.

"I have a feeling he's going to have me wrapped around his finger a lot sooner than I planned."

Denver lets out a belly laugh, which somehow eases my worries.

"Thanks for everything," I tell him, staring directly into his intense gaze.

He rolls his eyes and shoves my shoulder, but there is a playful grin on his face. "Stop thanking me and feed your boy."

I chuckle, and more of the anxious energy lifts from my chest. Denver has always had that effect on me.

That's what best friends are for, right?

At least, that's what he keeps telling me.

Once the bottle is ready, I set it on a table beside a rocking chair and rescue Sammy from his baby jail.

"Who's hungry?" I ask as I pick up the obviously upset infant and nestle him in the crook of my arm.

Once seated in the chair, I bring the bottle to his lips, which he instantly latches onto. I sigh and rock us back and forth while he eats.

It's still so crazy to me how tiny and perfect my son is.

I watch him as he drinks, letting all my worries disappear. When I glance up, Denver is staring at us. The expression on his face is hard to decipher, which isn't something I'm used to.

I know my best friend so well that sometimes it's as if I can read his mind. Although I'll admit, something changed this last year. He has put up a small wall between us. I don't think most people would notice the subtle change, but I have. I have to trust he will come to me when he's ready because something is clearly going on with him.

He doesn't realize I'm looking at him at first, but as soon as our gazes connect, his eyes go wide, and he quickly turns away.

"Lunch is almost ready," he calls over his shoulder, his voice slightly higher than it normally is, which sets off alarm bells in my brain.

What the fuck just happened?

Shaking my head, I turn my attention back to the tiny human in my arms. We're both running on the smallest amount of sleep. Heaven only knows when that is going to change. And sleep deprivation can lead to all kinds of problems.

I'm sure we will both experience oddities and shifts with all the changes taking place at once.

I'm the one who wanted this baby, yet Denver is putting in as much effort as I am.

"It's crazy how I'm responsible for an entire human now," I murmur, but I'm sure Denver can hear me.

"Life as we know it is changing forever," he replies. Then he tells me the food is ready.

Sammy takes a couple more minutes to finish his bottle, and once he's done, I put him on my shoulder to burp him. I cherish the few moments of cuddle time before my stomach rumbles, reminding me I also need to eat.

"You're going to spoil him if you hold him all the time," Denver mutters when I sit down to eat, but there is a hint of a smile on his lips that lets me know he doesn't mean it.

"I can eat a burger one-handed. Besides, maybe I want to spoil him," I counter with a raised brow and a smirk of my own.

"Well, if we are agreeing to spoil him, then hand him over," he says, reaching for my son. "I just finished eating, and I want my cuddle time."

I chuckle and pass Sammy over.

"He's so tiny," Denver whispers in a baby voice. It brings a smile to my face.

The past twenty-four hours might have been crazy, but a feeling of contentment washes over me.

I also can't help but notice how good Denver looks holding a baby. His eyes are focused solely on my son, and he appears as in love with him as I am. A weird sort of yearning forms in the pit of my stomach. It's an odd sensation, but I push it aside.

There isn't a safer place in this world for Sammy than in Denver's or my arms.

While I eat, I steal glances at my best friend holding my baby, and I'm not sure why. Anytime Denver catches me, he smiles, which reassures me that it's not weird to be watching, but something feels different.

I'm just not sure what.

It doesn't take long to finish my meal, and once I've cleaned up my dishes, I make a bottle for Sammy and steal him from Denver.

Natural light softly lights the nursery through the light curtains as I enter with my tiny baby in my arms. He greedily takes the bottle I offer him, and I relax into the rocking chair, savoring the moment. It's only when my own eyes start to flutter shut that I realize Sammy is done eating and almost asleep.

Since I forgot to change him before the bottle, I make quick work of cleaning his bum before laying him down. Thankfully, I didn't wake him too much. It would probably make more sense to change him first going forward.

This is all a learning curve for me.

As quietly as humanly possible, I shut the door behind me and almost jump when my eyes land on Denver leaning against the wall.

"You should nap," he suggests, clearly not caring that he almost gave me a heart attack.

I'm about to argue when a yawn slips past my lips. "Fine, but you should too," I counter as I study his face.

Dark circles shade beneath his gray eyes, and he looks like he's a few minutes from passing out.

"That's probably not a bad idea. I'll take the baby monitor with me," he states.

I furrow my brows. "You don't have to do that. I'm his father. I should be doing the brunt of the work with him."

Denver rolls his eyes and grabs the back of his neck. "You're such a stubborn ass. I told you the moment you found out about Sammy that

I would help. You don't have to do the majority of *anything*. We're in this together. Now stop arguing with me and go to sleep."

He steals the monitor from my hand and high-tails it to his room before I can protest. I'm too exhausted to argue and slide a hand over my face while turning to go to bed as I was commanded to do.

Denver may have called me a stubborn ass, but the same can be said for him. Maybe that's why we are best friends. We don't put up with each other's bullshit and call the other out when needed. He's been the one constant in my life. When others leave, Denver's always there.

He's been with me through every single milestone of my life, and I wouldn't want it any other way.

Every break-up, he was there.

Every missed opportunity, he was there.

When my parents died, and I was left broken and afraid, he was there.

Once my head hits the pillow, my eyes close, and I immediately fall asleep.

I'm not sure how long I sleep, but the smell of Denver's signature chili wakes me. I stretch my limbs before getting out of bed and making my way down the hall.

When I arrive at the kitchen-living room area, I'm pulled up short, my attention caught by the sight of Denver dancing with Sammy in his arms. A giant grin beams across his face as he stares at my son like he hung the moon. The sight makes my heart do a funny flip.

Shit, it's never done that for my best friend before. Maybe I didn't get enough sleep.

"How long was I out for?" I ask quietly, trying not to startle Denver, but by the way he gasps and pulls Sammy closer to his chest, it's clear I didn't succeed.

"You cops with your light feet," he grumbles, then kisses Sammy's head.

Again, my heart pulls. And how can it not? Denver is such a broad and masculine man, but the way he so carefully holds my precious baby is perfection. Man or woman, the sight is sure to do something to a person.

Maybe it's simply seeing how gentle and loving he is with my son that has me reacting this way. I don't know what else it could be. I've never been like this around him before, and the only new addition to our lives is Sammy. Something inside me is telling me that isn't quite right, but it isn't saying any more.

I shake my head, not ready to dwell on this at the moment, and move toward them and pull Sammy from Denver's arms for my own snuggles.

"I'd say a good four hours," Denver answers, and I'm surprised my eyebrows don't shoot through the roof.

"That long? It didn't feel like it."

Denver chuckles. "You obviously needed it."

"What about you?"

He shrugs. "I think I got a good hour before Little Man here woke demanding to be fed and changed." He uses his baby voice again as he finishes his sentence and boops Sammy on the nose.

"Well, at least you got something," I murmur, and Sammy squawks.

"He's probably hungry again. Why don't you change his bum first and swaddle him before giving him his bottle?" Denver suggests. "Maybe if we're lucky, he'll sleep for a few solid hours."

I nod, taking the baby to his room to do as I'm told.

As soon as I open the diaper, I gag. I don't do well with poop—never have. Blood is hit or miss, and vomit seems to be no problem since

I've had more than one person puke in the back of my cruiser, but shit, no way.

"How is someone so little so stinky?" I ask Sammy, quickly wiping his butt and throwing the diaper into the smell-proof garbage can beside the changing table.

Once he's clean and changed for the night, I lay a light blanket on the floor and place him in the middle like the nurse taught me. It takes me a couple of tries, but I finally get the swaddle perfect, and Sammy seems to love it. He's still smacking his lips, clearly wanting food, but he's not screaming, so that's a good thing.

"Ready for a bottle?" Denver asks, leaning against the doorframe with Sammy's formula in his hand.

"What would I do without you?" I whisper, looking into his eyes.

A flash of something sparks across his face, but he swiftly hides it behind that stupid emotional wall before walking over and handing me the bottle.

I wish he would talk to me.

I'm dying to know what he's hiding, but having known Denver for so long, I know better than to push him. He'll come to me when he's ready. It might take a long time, though.

"Good thing you'll never have to find out," he responds with a wink, then leaves.

My heart beats rapidly, and I wonder if I'm getting sick. Surely, it's not in response to the simple gesture. Denver has winked at me a million times before. It's something he does when he's teasing. *So why am I reacting differently today?*

Needing to clear my thoughts, I shift my focus to the tiny human depending on me. I gather him into my arms and sit in the ridiculously comfortable rocking chair.

The second the nipple is at his lips, he slurps it in greedily and drinks. Rocking him back and forth, I feed my precious baby and stare at his tiny face. I realize how much he resembles Samantha, from the tint of red in his fuzzy hair to the slender little nose and plush lips. It's obvious her genes were stronger than mine.

Sammy downs the bottle, and I place him on my shoulder to burp him while rocking. I hum a song my mom used to sing to me when I was little before she passed away. I'm not the best at carrying a tune, but I get through the song before Sammy falls asleep.

"I love you so much," I tell him as I rest him on his back in the crib.

"You okay?" Denver questions with furrowed brows when I enter the kitchen.

It's then I realize I was crying. I wipe my face hastily and shrug. "I was thinking about my mom. I guess I just miss her right now. It's moments like this she'd be a part of if she were here."

He nods as he walks toward me and places his hand on my shoulder. The touch is comforting, and I want to hug him for some reason.

Fuck it.

I pull Denver into my arms, and when he doesn't hug me back right away, I freak out a little. *Did I cross a line?* We're best friends, but we've never been overly physical with each other besides the bit of roughhousing and bro hugs here and there.

I think it comes from my parents both being more hands-off people. I used to hate it when my grandma would hug me, but it turns out sometimes you simply need a hug.

After a beat, Denver wraps his arms around me, squeezing tightly and holding me. And just like that, all of the worries melt away.

"Thanks for that," I murmur as I step back and wipe my face again. "Fuck, when did I turn into such a baby?"

"It's okay to cry," he assures me. "You're running on little sleep, and emotions are high right now. Besides, it doesn't make you a baby. Honestly, I think people who cry in front of others are strong as fuck. It's easy to hide behind a wall and keep things bottled up, but to show true vulnerability and let go... that takes strength."

I nod, and my stomach rumbles. It seems I've been doing a shit job of taking care of myself.

"Supper should be ready," Denver says with a tilt of his head. "I'm starving too."

As we're eating and bullshitting at the table, it dawns on me how perfect this all feels.

Why couldn't Denver be a woman?

Chapter Three

DENVER

"How's everything going?" Nixon, my boss and close friend, asks over the phone.

"Not bad. We all miss you, though," I respond, bringing out a good-hearted laugh from him.

"I call bullshit, but sure, we'll go with that," he mutters, and I chuckle.

"How are things in Brazil?" I question as I lean forward in my office chair and scroll through the emails in my inbox.

"A lot better than I thought. Dante's killing it at this role, and being in another country is keeping our minds off the shit waiting for us in the US."

I smile at the mention of his fiancé, the famous actor Dante Michaelson. That man has been through hell and back yet came out the other side stronger than ever. I have a lot of respect for him. His battles aren't over, but from how he's handled everything he's already been put through, he can make it through anything life throws at him.

"We'll all have your backs when the time comes," I remind him.

Dante's father is a psycho pastor who emotionally abused him throughout his entire life, going as far as having someone drug Dante simply to have things align with his fucked-up agenda. And his own mother hit him with a car after stalking him outside a store. We're waiting for the trial to happen in a few months to see if the courts agree that his father should be locked up. His mother already took a plea bargain and is serving her sentence.

"How are the new clients working out?" he asks, bringing the conversation to work again.

"Really good. Nothing too crazy to report. I hate being mostly behind the desk right now, though," I complain.

"Don't I know that, but with everything Dante and I have planned, being more behind the scenes is going to work out well for me," he responds.

Is he hinting at what I think he is?

"Can we speed up the next two and a half months so you can take over this role, and I can be back in the field?" I joke.

"But then you wouldn't be home every night to spend with Ford and the baby," he reminds me. "How are they doing, by the way?"

I smile, thinking of my best friend and the cutest little boy around. "Both Ford and I are exhausted, but Sammy is growing every day. I can't believe he's already a week old."

"I hear time flies with kids," he muses.

"It really does. I'm sure you'll find out one day," I tease, knowing Nixon and Dante want babies one day.

"Make sure you're taking care of yourself. I wish we were there to help you guys out."

"The rest of the crew has been a ton of help, almost too much. By the number of dishes I have in my freezer, you'd think my friends forgot I know how to cook," I joke.

Nixon laughs. "I'm glad they are taking care of you guys. If you need to work from home, don't be afraid to do that," he states in a dominant tone.

"I will. So far, everything is going okay, but it is only my second day back. We'll see how it goes. What I'm more nervous about is when

Ford goes back to work in three weeks. I don't know if I trust someone to keep Sammy safe," I admit.

Even though Ford could technically get twelve weeks of paternity leave, it would be unpaid, and although he hates the idea of leaving his son, he doesn't want to be unable to offer financial support for that long.

"You can bring him to the office if you want," Nixon offers. "I obviously wouldn't recommend bringing a baby into the field, but for the time being, I don't see why you couldn't have him with you."

A sense of immediate relief washes over me. I was unaware of how much anxiety I was carrying over this.

"I'll talk to Ford about it, but that sounds amazing. Sophy and Margret would love to have baby snuggles if I needed to have a client meeting," I reply, mentioning our tech specialist and secretary.

Nixon laughs. "That they would. I'm surprised Sophy and Slate haven't had babies of their own yet."

I hate having discussions about other people's families because so much happens behind closed doors. It's no one else's business.

My mom was someone who loved babies and had trouble conceiving. She told me how it would bother her when people asked when she was going to start a family. And when you're trying to have a baby, it only adds to the stress.

After she had my older sister, Kelly, it took her almost seven years to have me.

"If it's meant to be, it will be," I respond.

"True. Anyway, I should go. Dante needs to get to set soon," he says, then shares a quick goodbye and ends the call.

As soon as I hang up, my phone starts ringing again, and I shake my head when I see my mom's picture. It's almost as if thinking about the woman summoned her to call.

"Hey, Mom," I answer with a smile.

"Don't 'hey, Mom' me. You haven't called me in almost a week. How is that precious baby doing?"

I chuckle. "He's doing awesome. Not sleeping worth a darn, but he's cute, so it helps."

Mom laughs and then sighs. "Are you sure you don't want me to come out there for a bit and help out?"

"We've got it, Mom, but thanks for the offer. Besides, Madison and Nelly would miss you too much," I remind her.

My sister moved across the country a year after she graduated high school to go to college. Unfortunately for my mom, she fell in love and stayed where she was. Once Ford and I were settled into our careers and lives, she moved out to be with them and help with their kids.

After Ford's parents passed away, my mom took him under her wing and raised him like another son. Ford's grandparents were technically his legal guardians but were more than happy for my mom to raise him for those last four years until he turned eighteen. It was super cool to get to live under the same roof in high school. It brought us even closer.

Although the feelings I've had for him the last year are not brotherly at all. At first, I felt guilty about it, but I've come to accept it for what it is.

As long as no one knows about these feelings, no one can get hurt.

"You're not wrong there. But those two angels know they are my world," Mom says, stopping me from dwelling on the things I can't change.

My nieces are spoiled rotten, but my mother wouldn't have it any other way.

"Even if you don't want my help, I'm still coming out in a few weeks to meet that precious little boy," she reminds me as if I could forget about her planned trip.

After confirming that I'll pick her up from the airport at the end of the month, we hang up, and I spend a good chunk of time responding to emails and scheduling people where they need to be for the week.

Once those tasks are taken care of, I log into Amazon and start shopping for baby things for my office. I'm sure Ford will be on board with the plan Nixon suggested, so I add the supplies I'll need to my cart and checkout.

"Honey, I'm home," I tease as I walk through the door.

"Supper's almost ready, *babe*," Ford teases with a wink that makes my heart flutter.

Fuck, I shouldn't have started the joke.

"Look who's awake," I coo at Sammy to distract myself from yearning for my best friend.

He makes a face, and I yelp with joy. "He smiled at me!" I shout, which startles the little man, his limbs flinging everywhere and his eyes going wide.

"It was probably just gas," Ford replies, and I stick my tongue out at him.

"Don't steal my joy," I grumble, picking up Sammy and bouncing him gently in my arms. "Did you miss me?" I ask in a baby voice. "I missed you."

"How was work?" Ford asks after a few minutes of my babbling at the bundle of joy.

"Boring, but I have some good news," I inform him with a toothy grin.

Ford stares at me with a raised brow as if to say *Are you going to spit it out?*

"Nixon suggested I could bring Sammy to work with me once you go back to work, so we don't have to worry about childcare just yet."

"Was he serious?" he asks, running his hand through his blond hair.

"Absolutely. I already ordered a playpen for the office and some supplies I can leave there so we aren't bringing stuff back and forth so much."

He blows out a breath and smiles.

"Shit, I didn't realize how stressed I was about finding a good childcare provider," he replies.

I chuckle with a nod. "I felt the same way. It was like a weight was lifted off my shoulders when Nixon brought up the idea of bringing Sammy with me. I don't know how we're ever supposed to trust a stranger with this perfect little person." My voice changes at the end as I direct the words more toward Sammy.

"Do you realize how much you use that baby voice?" Ford asks.

"He likes it," I respond dryly.

He laughs. "Whatever helps the big macho bodyguard sleep at night," he jokes, and I chuckle along.

"Did you get a nap in at all today?" I question, noticing how dark and deep the circles under his eyes are.

Ford shakes his head and blows out a breath. "I tried to, but Sammy decided he was only going to power nap a bunch today instead of getting in solid blocks. The one time he slept for a longer block, Melody called. I might have to go back to work sooner than we planned."

He looks defeated, and I can't help but feel sorry for him.

"How much sooner?" I question, a knot forming in my stomach. Four weeks was already not a long time.

"Next week," he murmurs, and I almost gasp. That's two weeks ahead of schedule.

His partner wouldn't request he come back early if it wasn't an emergency, but still, I hate that he'll miss out on more of Sammy's early days because of it.

"Well, at least we have the childcare situation figured out," I point out as a positive. "How 'bout I take the monitor tonight so you can catch up on sleep?" I suggest as he reaches for the plates.

"You don't have to do that," he states, and I want to punch him.

"Stop fighting me on every aspect of this." My tone leaves no room for argument. "We're a team. That means we do this fifty-fifty. Nixon also said I was allowed to work from home when needed. I'll send an email right away letting the team know that it will be happening tomorrow. If I need to take a nap tomorrow, I can."

He stares intently into my eyes for a few beats before closing his and nodding.

"Thank you," he whispers.

"It's what friends are for."

Sometimes, when I let my mind wander, I wish we could be more than friends. That he'd have a late-in-life bi-awakening too, but hoping for something like that is dangerous. I have to be content with what we have.

Sammy starts to make little noises, and I'm thankful for the distraction.

"When did he eat last?" I ask.

Ford picks up his phone, looking at the log he keeps. "A while ago. It's probably time for another bottle, and considering how weird his sleep was today, you might be able to get him down for a few hours now."

"Perfect. You finish dinner, and I'll take care of this little guy. By the time we're both done, we can eat and bullshit about our days."

"Sounds like a plan," he responds, and when he turns away, I start making a bottle.

The way we are falling into easy routines has me wishing this could be a forever thing. But one day, Ford isn't going to need me anymore, and I'll just be watching his life from the sidelines.

Chapter Four

FORD

SAMMY SCREAMS HIS LUNGS out while I rock him back and forth, and I feel hopeless.

"Shh... you're okay," I whisper, but it doesn't make him stop.

His diaper is dry, he's had a bottle, and he let out a good burp after he ate. Yet every time I lay him down for his nap, he lets out a piercing cry.

What am I doing wrong here?

Sammy is eleven days old today, and his sleep isn't getting any better. He seems grumpy most of the time, and I can't figure out what to do. It probably doesn't help that I'm also running on fumes.

Denver offered to take the monitor last night since I've had it for the past three nights, but I refused. He has a job he needs to be able to function for. Maybe I'll think differently when I return to work, but this should be on me for now. Sammy is my son. *My* responsibility. It isn't right to make Denver take on too much. I don't care how much he keeps telling me we're in this together.

Besides, I don't sleep well if I can't check the baby monitor one last time before closing my eyes. And I'm not sure if that is ever going to change.

The reason I'm fighting his help so much is the fact that he has stepped back from his social life. It makes me feel guilty for relying on him, even though I do need him. We were both hopeful we'd be able to handle this, but with how difficult Sammy has been, I figured Denver would be pulling away.

Yes, we're best friends and closer than most people are, but he's a single guy. He should be out there finding himself a woman to love. Instead, he's spending his nights with my baby, who cries all the time, and me. It eats at me, yet I can't bring myself to force him out of the house either.

I like that we've been relaxing on the couch at the end of the day. Being in his presence casts this net of comfort over me and has me yearning for even more time with him. I almost hate when we separate at night to our own bedrooms, which is weird, but I can't stop the feeling, though I don't want to analyze it either. It's the same with how my heart flutters and warms watching him with Sammy.

Sammy is a handful, and I've been fighting Denver tooth and nail, but he isn't letting me push him away. And that only adds to the guilt. There aren't enough words in the world to thank him for all he's been doing for us.

This leaves me with the question I've been thinking about every day since we got home from the hospital. *How the hell am I supposed to do this on my own?*

At some point, I'm going to have to. It's not fair to him to have to take all of this on. I'm sure he's only doing all of it out of a sense of obligation. I know he says he wants to, but nothing about this is supposed to be permanent. If I don't get my shit together sooner rather than later, he's going to grow to resent me.

Sammy is still screaming, so I switch to a gentle bounce in my arms as tears brim at my eyes.

"How long has he been crying for?" Denver asks.

I jump, clinging Sammy to my chest as I gasp for air. "Shit. What are you doing here?"

"Sorry, didn't mean to scare you. I texted you an hour ago, letting you know I'd be home for lunch."

I nod, but at this point, I'm delirious with exhaustion and frustration. "I've been in here with Mr. Man for a while. I guess I didn't hear it." A yawn slips past my lips.

"When did *you* sleep last?" he interrogates me.

"What is sleep?" I joke, trying to lighten the mood, but the glare I'm receiving from Denver tells me he's not going to let this go.

Stepping forward with determination, he takes Sammy from my arms and points out the door. "Go to bed," he commands. "I'll work from home for the rest of the afternoon."

I shake my head, wanting to argue, but Denver's expression turns deadly.

"Don't even think about arguing," he snarls, and I'm taken aback. "You look like you're about to drop dead, Ford. I've never seen you like this before. You're no good to your son if you pass out. Take the fucking help I'm offering you."

As much as I hate to admit it, Denver is right. I'm only moments from passing out from pure exhaustion. I don't have the energy to fight him. We can talk more about things later.

Slumping my shoulders, I sluggishly pad to my bedroom, closing the door behind me. Within seconds of my head hitting the pillow, sleep pulls me under, and reality is quickly replaced with the dream world.

A warm body is in front of me, close but not close enough, so I reach out to pull them into me. Once their body is nestled perfectly against mine, I kiss their neck and shoulder before pulling their earlobe into my mouth.

I'm not sure who this is, but their throaty moans tell me they are as into this as I am.

My cock throbs between my legs, and I thrust aginst the ass of my bed partner, needing some friction.

I'm not a selfish lover, so I reach around their torso to grab a breast but am confused when my hand lands on a solid, muscular chest. That's when I notice the moans coming from the person in front of me are deeper than I'm used to. But I don't stop.

Again, I thrust aginst the firm ass of the man in my grasp, and he lets out a gravelly groan.

As if acting on its own accord, my hand snakes down his torso, landing on his rock-hard cock and giving it a long, firm tug.

"Fuck," he breathes out in a sex-laced voice, which makes my cock bob between my legs against him. "I need more," he pleads.

"What do you need?" I ask, not knowing how to please a man.

"Fuck me," he begs. "I'm so ready for you."

I swallow a lump that has formed in my throat, but I don't reject his request. Instead, I grab the bottle of lube and a condom from the nightstand and squirt some onto my fingers. Only when I move to stretch him do I find he's wearing a butt plug.

Clearly, he meant he was ready.

With a gentle yet firm tug, I pull it free, then the man moves onto all fours while I sheath myself and lather my throbbing erection in lube. Once I'm good and slick, I position myself behind him and slowly slide in. His hot, tight channel chokes my cock, and it takes everything not to blow my load within seconds.

"So... good..." the man murmurs between heavy pants.

Good isn't the right word to describe this experience, though. Otherworldly, fucking perfection, absolutely mind-blowing—those are much better descriptors for what I am experiencing. Good isn't enough, but, of course, I don't tell him that. Instead, I focus on getting the entire length of my cock into his perfect body.

His shoulder blades flex as I slide into him, and I run a hand up and down his muscular back, taking in his perfect body.

Once I've finally bottomed out, I lean over his body to kiss his neck, but he turns his head to claim my mouth.

Normally, when I kiss a partner, my eyes are closed, but for some reason, I keep them open this time. I'm expecting nameless eyes I've never seen before, not the piercing gray ones I've looked into a million times before.

As if realizing I'm fucking my best friend is sensory overload for my brain, I come with a roar.

"Wake up." A deep, gravelly voice cuts through the fog as my body shakes. But it's not moving on its own. No, the person talking is shaking me.

My heart is racing when I groggily open my eyes.

What kind of fucking dream was that?

Denver is sitting on the edge of the bed with Sammy in his arms. The look of concern on his face makes me panic even more.

Was I doing anything in my sleep to show what I was dreaming about? Did I say anything?

"What time is it?" I ask with a shaky voice as I sit up, keeping the covers firmly on top of me and praying my dream wood isn't too evident. It's crazy that I'm still hard when I should be anything but.

"Almost three," Denver supplies, still eying me up in a funny way, but he doesn't say whatever it is he's thinking. "I booked Sammy a doctor's appointment for four, so I need you to get up and put on some clean clothes," he instructs. "I was hoping to get us in tomorrow, but the pediatrician had either today or next week. Since Sammy's so uncomfortable, I didn't want to wait that long."

I clench my jaw before blowing out a breath. My cock quickly deflates, and I hate myself a little right now.

Why didn't I think to make a doctor's appointment? Did I make a mistake wanting a baby?

Clearly, I'm failing as a father.

"Thanks," I murmur and get out of bed, not having to worry about giving Denver an eyeful anymore.

"I'll get Mr. Man ready and meet you in the living room," he tells me as he walks away but pauses at the door. "And brush your teeth. Your breath stinks," he teases with a wink, then leaves the room.

How is it a simple joke can lighten the mood so easily?

Maybe the look of concern on his face earlier didn't have anything to do with me and was all about Sammy. I don't have time to think about it or decipher the dream.

I need to focus on my son right now, so I hurry to get ready.

After I brush my teeth, I join Denver and Sammy in the living room, where, of course, Denver has thought of everything. The diaper bag hangs off his shoulder, and Little Man is only somewhat fussy in his car seat, ready to go.

As much as I *hate* that Denver is helping me so much, I'm also incredibly thankful he's here.

"Do you need to check my breath? I brushed," I tease, but it almost feels forced. That dream is seriously fucking with my head.

Something passes in Denver's eyes, and if I weren't still so tired, I would think it was heat. But surely that's not the case. Clearly, my fucked-up brain is playing tricks on me.

He clears his throat and says, "Haha. You ready?"

Since he already has Sammy situated, I grab my wallet and keys, offering to drive. It might not be much, but I feel like I'm doing something. It will also give me something to focus on.

Before I can even get us out of the driveway, Sammy is fast asleep. Glancing in the rearview mirror, Denver appears to be dozing off as well, so I let him catch a few minutes. With a fussy baby, we need to get whatever sleep we can. And with my best friend dozing, I don't have to worry about acting normal. It gives me some time to gather my thoughts and calm my anxious heart.

What does a dream like that mean?

Obviously, I've had sex dreams before, but never about a man, and damn sure never about my best friend. *Is it possible it's just sleep deprivation messing with my head?*

Denver has been a constant help and there for me more than ever since Sammy arrived. Maybe that's why he was in my dream, and it doesn't have to mean more than that.

Neither of them stirs even through the stop-and-go traffic and noisy city. I can't help but steal glances along the way, still feeling confused yet blessed at the same time.

"We're here," I whisper as I pull into the parking lot, not wanting to wake my son.

Denver's eyes flutter open, and he wipes his chin with the back of his hand. "We're here? Man, I must have fallen asleep right away."

"You did, and I'm glad. Think we can get him inside without waking him?"

I'm not taking any chances, not when he is finally resting.

"I got him. Just don't let your door slam," he cautions as he slips out of the back seat, sliding the car seat with him.

"Thank you. Seriously. Those words aren't enough to express how grateful I am for you," I tell him as we walk inside the clinic.

He simply smiles, which causes butterflies to erupt in my stomach, and it has me wondering if I need to ask the doctor about symptoms of sleep deprivation. I'm clearly staring at him for too long when he clears his throat and says, "I've got Mr. Man here. Go get him checked in."

I shake my head with an awkward chuckle at his directions and rush to get Sammy checked in before joining them.

Denver and I idly chat as we wait to get called in, and I try my hardest not to make things awkward.

"Did you sleep all right?" he asks.

My brow shoots up, and I almost feel like I've been punched in the stomach. "Um... yeah... why?"

"You were whimpering in your sleep, and I was worried you were having a nightmare," he informs me. "Did you not notice that you were covered in sweat when you woke up?"

Instant relief washes over me at his words. He didn't clue into what kind of dream it was. That's a plus.

"I did notice the sweat, but I don't remember the dream," I lie, which leaves a ball of guilt that feels like lead in my stomach.

I *never* lie to Denver. But now is *not* the time for the truth. I don't know when that time will be.

Thankfully, we are called into a room then, and I can focus on something other than these mixed-up feelings.

When Dr. Lize comes in, she asks us a bunch of questions as she checks Sammy over. Her warm smile is comforting, but I'm still worried about how fussy the tiny little man has been. I hate seeing him cry all the time.

"I think Sammy has acid reflux," she tells us when she's finished her exam.

"I didn't know babies could get that," I respond.

She nods with a soft smile. "It's actually pretty common. There are a few things you can do to minimize the reflux, like holding Sammy in a more upright position while feeding him, feeding him smaller amounts more frequently, and taking extra time to burp after feeding. However, it sounds like you've already been doing a lot of that. Thankfully, reflux can also be treated with a medication that has very little side effects. We'll keep the dose the same so as he grows, it will actually become a lesser dose. Most grow out of it by a year, but we can reassess him when he gets there."

She prints off the prescription, and I pray it works.

"It can take a few days for the medication to work, but if nothing has changed in a week, please bring him back," she advises.

I nod along, but the exhaustion catches up to me again, and I feel disconnected from my body.

"How are you doing?" she asks me.

"Babies are hard," I reply nonchalantly.

"Have you been getting enough sleep?"

Man, I feel like I'm being interrogated.

"Does any parent get enough sleep?" I counter sharply with a raised brow.

"I'm just trying to help."

I sigh, feeling guilty for going on the defense so quickly.

"It's hard right now. I feel like I'm barely hanging on, but I know I'll get through it. It just takes time, right?"

With Denver in the room, I can't bring myself to ask about weird dreams.

"Sometimes. Other times, it could be something more. Since Sammy has been rather colicky, you could just be experiencing the baby blues, which can cause mood swings, crying spells, anxiety, and difficulty sleeping."

"Can nightmares be a side effect of that?" Denver asks, which has me feeling guilty again because *I* know it wasn't a nightmare.

Dr. Lize nods. "Absolutely. Sleep deprivation can lead to more intense, vivid dreams and nightmares."

Those words put an ease to the anxiety I've been having about the dream. It's nice to know it was simply the lack of sleep.

"Have you been experiencing those?" she questions both of us.

"I woke up sweaty after my nap, and apparently, I was whimpering in my sleep," I admit.

"I'm just concerned about him," Denver adds, which warms me a little.

"That's normal. Both of your lives have been completely changed. How about we touch base in a few weeks to see how you're all doing?"

I nod. "I can do that."

"I'll make sure we're here, and this one doesn't try to get out of it," Denver pipes up, elbowing me.

Dr. Lize smiles. "It's great you have a support system. That helps a lot. Make sure you continue to lean on those who are there for you," she tells me before leaving the room.

Her words hit me directly in the chest. I've been fighting Denver's support out of guilt, but the doctor is telling me to embrace it. I guess I'll have to trust that my best friend won't grow to resent me, and he *actually* wants to be there for me.

Denver insisted on driving home, and thankfully, Sammy slept through most of it.

I'll admit, I'm pretty sure I dozed off after we picked up the prescription. I swear, no matter how much sleep I get, I still feel completely exhausted.

When does that end?

"Want to help me with bath time?" I ask Denver as we walk through the doors.

"You're actually asking for help? Did hell freeze over?" he jokes.

I huff out a dry laugh before giving him an apologetic look. "I'm sorry I've been an asshole. I'm just worried you're going to resent me. You didn't sign up to help parent a baby who cries all the time and never sleeps."

"Dude. Babies cry," he counters. "Especially when they aren't feeling well. That's no one's fault. Besides, I knew what I was signing on for. I'm here to help with whatever life throws your way. That's what best friends do. I'm in this for the long haul, Ford. As long as you need me, I'm here."

I blink back a few tears wanting to break free, something that seems to be happening a lot lately. I guess I'll blame it on the baby blues for now.

Sammy makes a noise in his car seat, reminding us he needs our attention.

"Who's ready for a bath?" I coo to my son, and he makes another noise I'm taking to mean *I am*.

"I'll get the water to the right temperature. You change Sammy's bum and get him naked," Denver states.

I'm already crouching down to release the tiny man from his car seat, so I lean my shoulder into Denver's leg, giving him a playful shove. "Sure, take the easy job."

He chuckles. "Just make sure if you vomit, you don't do it on the carpet."

Laughter bubbles out of me as I tread down the hall to Sammy's room.

"Let's get you cleaned," I babble to the cutest boy in the entire world as I strip him out of his onesie.

Thankfully, I only gag a tiny bit when I change his diaper. When we're all done, I take my naked baby to the bathroom.

When I walk in, Denver says, "Water's fine. Come on in," holding his hands out for Sammy.

He's kneeling beside the tub on a mat that's cushioned to prevent our knees from hurting like a son of a bitch. I was beyond fortunate for the purchase the first time we bathed him.

Once Sammy is safe in Denver's arms, I lean against the counter, watching him gently place the squirming baby into the warm water. The second Sammy is in his baby tub, he relaxes, and I smile.

"He loves the water," I note.

"I mean, what's not to love?" he responds with a cheeky grin, pouring a dollop of baby wash onto a face cloth.

Instead of pushing Denver out of the way like I want to, I stay still and watch. He's treating Sammy with the same gentle care I do, which makes my heart do that funny flippy thing it's been doing the past week.

My best friend obviously loves my son as much as I do. It's because Denver is more than my best friend. He's family.

While Denver is singing to Sammy as he washes him, it dawns on me why women say it's hot when men take care of a baby. I'm straight, yet I'm a little attracted to my best friend right now.

Is that normal? Am I still having mixed feelings from the dream?

"What?" Denver asks, pulling me from my odd thoughts and making me wonder if I said that out loud.

I blink a few times. "What?" I repeat, and he chuckles.

"You're staring. I'm just wondering if my ass is hanging out or something?" he jokes, then turns his attention back to Sammy, using a cup to rinse his hair.

I *wasn't* staring at his ass before, but at the mention of it, my eyes zero in. *Have I ever noticed how nice his butt is before?* It's round and firm and a lot bigger than mine. His shirt is riding up, showing off a sliver of his olive skin and strong back. I bite my lip before I realize what's happening.

Shit, I'm checking out my best friend.

"I'm going to get Sammy a towel," I call out, rushing out of the bathroom, panic racing down my spine like an icy shower.

Once I'm safely out of sight, I lean against the wall and take a few deep breaths to calm my racing heart. *What the hell is wrong with me?*

First, it was the dream, now I'm staring at my best friend's ass, and from the bulge in my pants, I more than liked it. Straight men don't do that, so what does that make me? Is it possible this is all from the lack of sleep? Or is it more than that?

Taking a few slow breaths to calm myself, I think of shitty diapers, math equations, my grandma in a bathtub—anything to get my erection to deflate. Then I grab a hooded towel and head back to the bathroom.

I will have to examine these random feelings at some point because they are getting harder to justify with excuses.

But my son comes first.

Chapter Five

DENVER

FORD KEEPS LOOKING AT me funny, which is weirding me the fuck out. I'm not sure what is going on in his head, but honestly, it started after his nap. It got a little better after the doctor's appointment, but it started up again in the bathroom and has continued throughout the evening.

If I didn't know him better, I'd say he checked me out a few times, but that can*not* be right.

I'm deep in thought while cleaning the kitchen when Ford sits at the island, startling me a little. "How'd bedtime go?" I ask, wiping down the counter.

"Not bad. I think keeping him upright longer after he ate definitely helped."

"That's good. Maybe he'll sleep a bit better tonight," I reply as I drape the cloth over the faucet and turn toward him.

"That would be *amazing*. I'm not functioning on such little sleep," Ford admits, but I'm already aware of that.

"Let me take the monitor tonight. I'm off tomorrow anyway, so I don't even have to work from home."

He presses his lips together briefly before nodding. I almost gasp at how easily he accepted my help. Who knew all I needed to get Ford to stop fighting me was a doctor's agreement?

"Want to watch a movie before we hit the hay?" I suggest, wanting to spend a little more time with him before we go to sleep. Maybe I'll be able to get him to tell me what's going on in his head.

"Sure, why not?" He smiles. "Got anything in mind?"

"Not really, but would you mind if we watched it in one of our rooms? My back is out. Relaxing in bed might be a bit more comfortable."

I'm not sure it's a great idea, considering how my feelings have been growing for him, but sitting on the couch for too long is going to kill me, and then I won't be able to help Ford out tomorrow, and I'd hate that even more.

"Sure, but make sure you book a chiropractor appointment," he reminds me.

I can't help but laugh because I've been the one worrying about him and Sammy, but clearly, I've been forgetting about myself. "Yes, *Mom*," I tease.

Ford flips me the bird, which results in us both laughing as we head to our rooms to change into more comfortable clothing.

Once I'm ready, I make my way to Ford's door and enter without knocking, something I've done a million times before. But I quickly step back, hitting my head on the wall at the sight in front of me. I was not expecting him to still be getting dressed.

"Shit," I curse, grabbing my head.

Ford gasps, wearing only a pair of gray sweatpants. They hang low on his hips, showing off that delicious V and carved abs. A light spackling of hair trails down his stomach, pointing to forbidden treasure. My mouth goes dry, and I can't stop staring at him. Almost too soon, he pulls on a shirt, covering his tempting body.

"Forget how to walk?" he teases, but the words sound forced.

I scoff once I'm able to move again, acting like it's no big deal when it is. "Just figured you'd be dressed by now. Didn't realize you were so old that it took you extra time, and I wasn't expecting to see your ugly body," I lie.

"I'd take offense if I didn't know, without a doubt, my body is not ugly," Ford replies. "And if I'm old, so are you. We are the same age. I bet you're just jealous that your abs aren't as nice as mine." He's joking and now sounds a bit more like he normally does.

Something happened this afternoon, and I wish he would tell me what's going on.

"Whatever helps you sleep at night," I mutter, carefully climbing onto the bed.

"I know we said a movie, but I was wondering if you wanted to watch a comedy special instead?" he asks as he pulls up a streaming service.

"Sounds good to me," I tell him with a shrug, knowing that no matter what he puts on, it won't have my full attention.

Ford gently lowers himself onto the bed beside me, his arm brushing against mine as he gets comfortable. Goose bumps break out across my skin, and I fight the urge to suck in air.

His wide ocean eyes dart to mine with confusion painted across them.

Does he feel something too?

"Need any extra pillows?" he asks after clearing his throat and glancing away.

I inhale deeply and shake my head. "I'm good," I murmur, and he nods, keeping his focus solely on the television.

An awkward air fills the room. *What should I say to break the ice?*

"I saw this guy when I was scrolling social media the other day. He's fucking hilarious," Ford pipes up after pressing play.

"Perfect," I respond as the show starts.

The comedy is a good distraction from the sexy man lying next to me. However, it's not enough to keep my eyes open. Not too long later, sleep pulls me under.

I'm unsure how long I'm asleep when tiny whimpers wake me. Fluttering my eyes open, I remember I'm not in my room. But the fact that I fell asleep in Ford's bed isn't what has my eyes jolting wide. It's the realization that my best friend is holding me in his arms.

My heart races. *Is this just a dream?* It wouldn't be the first time I've dreamed of Ford. But his fingers twitch against my stomach where my shirt rode up, and his sleepy breath whispers against my neck, making me extremely aware that this is real.

I stay still at first, trying to figure out what to do, when Ford's hips move, pressing his crotch into my ass. My dick perks up at the movement.

I have to get out of here this very moment.

I'm sure Ford's sleep-filled brain thinks I'm Samantha, and that's why he's cuddling me. But my cock thinks differently, growing in my sweats. If my best friend wakes up now, there will be no hiding how excited I'm getting.

Sammy squawks again, reminding me why I'm awake in the first place.

As gently as possible, I pull away from the warm embrace of my best friend and tiptoe out of the room after picking up the baby monitor to bring with me. Thankfully, Ford doesn't stir, and I'm able to escape without an awkward and embarrassing conversation.

I quickly warm up a bottle of formula before rescuing the tiny little man from his baby jail and changing his bum. Once his diaper is clean, I cuddle him in my arms and feed him his bottle.

"Little Man, I'm not sure what I'm going to do about my feelings for your father," I whisper to the precious baby as he guzzles down his formula.

It would be nice if Sammy could talk and give me some advice, but he stays silent while drinking his milk, staring at me with innocent green eyes.

"Good talk," I mutter as he spits out the bottle, and I lift him to pat his back.

My feelings for Ford are growing. I'm not sure how long I will be able to keep things a secret.

I want to tell him how I feel, but there is no way he feels the same way. And the idea of losing my best friend over this terrifies me.

Chapter Six

FORD

DENVER WAS IN MY arms. It must have been a dream, but it felt so fucking real, which has my brain racing. Last time, I knew it was a dream. This time, I could have sworn he was actually next to me. Honestly, I can still smell him on my pillow, but that must be from when we were hanging out. I'm not sure when he left because I'm not even positive when I fell asleep.

I stretch my arms over my head as the memory of my second confusing dream replays in my head.

Yesterday afternoon, I had a dream about fucking my best friend, then last night, I got hard by staring at his ass, and now I had a dream about holding him.

Straight guys *don't* do that.

So what does that make me?

My heart races as I lie in bed, trying to figure out what to do. I wish I had someone to talk to about this, but the guy I normally reach out to for everything is why I feel like this.

What is he going to say when I tell him? Is he going to be upset? I know he won't care that I'm bi or whatever I am, but he might not like that he's the reason I'm coming to this realization. Even if he's not upset, will things between us be weird? Am I going to have to find a new place to live?

My body aches as the panic of all of this takes over.

I've always liked having a small social circle, but now I feel like that's coming to bite me in the ass. I want someone I can turn to right now who maybe would understand, but no one comes to mind. Melody, my partner, would take a call and listen, but she wouldn't have any words of advice, which is what I'm in desperate need of right now.

I'm thirty-eight fucking years old, and I'm suddenly attracted to my best friend. Is that normal? *If I'm not straight, what am I?* Doubt and confusion are on a constant loop.

"Fuck," I grumble, running a hand over my face.

Closing my eyes, I force myself to take a deep inhale and slowly blow it out. I repeat the motion a few times until my heart rate slows. Once the panic has subsided, I do a self-check-in. *What am I really freaking out about?*

My gut is telling me that my sexuality isn't the cause. Thinking I'm not straight anymore doesn't seem like a big deal. It feels like I've peeled back a new layer of myself, but it doesn't feel wrong.

What's freaking me out the most is the idea of straining my relationship with Denver. He's always been my constant. He's the one I turn to for *everything*. I don't know what I'd do without him. Even if things were only a tiny bit different because of this, I would hate it. I don't want to be the cause of hurting our relationship in any way, but I also don't want to keep this from him.

This is *huge* for me, and I want him to know. Maybe I'll just leave out the part about him, but I'm not sure that will be good enough. He should know how I feel. I hate lying to him.

Since I have no one else to talk to about something crazy like this, I decide to turn to the internet.

After grabbing my phone off the nightstand, I Google '*figuring out your sexuality late in life*' and come across a shit ton of articles. I scroll through a few, finding out I'm not alone.

A lot of people have discovered they are bi, gay, pan, demi, or other things at a wide range of ages. Some of my anxiety eases as I read through people's stories, but the confusion remains. I never expected to be having this awakening at this point in my life.

What do I do about this?

I know I need to tell Denver, but how does one exactly bridge this conversation? Do I simply blurt out, *"You have a really nice ass, and I was wondering if maybe you wanted to experiment with me?"* I can imagine how well that would go over.

Denver has never hinted at being anything but straight, and I would hate for this to ruin our friendship. So I'm back to the idea of only bringing up my sexual confusion and leaving his name out of it so we can have a conversation.

Denver isn't homophobic, so if I were to explain this to him, he wouldn't stop being friends with me, but again, I'm left with this annoying feeling that it could make things awkward, especially if he started asking questions about *how* I figured this out. I refuse to lie to him anymore, but I'm not sure how I would deal with things if he distanced himself from me because of the truth.

Why does this have to be so fucking complicated?

And why now, *of all times, am I peeling back this new layer of myself?*

Life is already chaotic as it is with a newborn, but now I'm risking losing part of my support system.

Sighing, I drop my phone onto the bed beside me and throw my head against the pillow.

Knowing I don't want to hide this, I focus on coming up with a game plan to tell my best friend I'm pretty sure I'm not straight.

I lie still for a while, going over a million different scenarios in my head. None of them are putting me one hundred percent at ease, but staying in bed any longer feels stupid. It's not like I'm going to sleep anymore.

I kick my legs over the edge, get up, and pad down the hall to the kitchen, where the delicious smell of bacon lures me.

"Smells great," I call out.

Denver beams at me over his shoulder. *Why didn't I notice just how perfect his smile is until right now?*

"Should be ready in five minutes," he tells me.

I nod and head over to where Sammy sits in a vibrating bouncy chair, happy for the distraction. If it weren't for my son, I might have spent too long staring at my best friend, then he'd totally clue in something was off.

"Do you like watching Denver cook?" I coo at Sammy, and he makes an expression that's really close to a smile. "Shit, he really does smile."

Denver laughs and points at me. "See! I fucking told you."

"What time did he wake you up?" I ask as I tickle Sammy's tiny foot.

"Early," Denver grumbles but doesn't look upset. "He was up a few times throughout the night like regular too, but I got him back down quickly."

"How did I not hear any of that?" I question as I head for the coffee pot to pour myself a cup. "Do you want some more?"

Denver nods with a giant grin. "That would be amazing," he says with a tired sigh.

"It's nice out today," I point out, staring at the bright blue sky through the kitchen window. "I should take Sammy for a walk after breakfast. If you're not too tired, you could join us," I suggest, then take a sip of my coffee.

"That sounds nice. We'll get to test out that expensive stroller I bought."

I smirk and shake my head. "I doubt that thing is going to be worth the price you paid for it."

"Oh ye of little faith," he says, and I chuckle.

It doesn't take long for Denver to finish cooking. All the while, I keep wondering if he notices how awkward I'm feeling as we sit side by side to eat.

I'm participating in the conversation as much as I can, but my focus is solely on the man beside me.

I take in the way his jaw moves as he chews, how his Adam's apple bobs when he swallows, how his eyes soften when he talks to Sammy, and the fact his entire face lights up when my son does something cute, which is often.

How have I gone so long without noticing all these things, and why am I suddenly so fixated on him? My head is spinning, but I can't figure out how to bring up these feelings, not yet, anyway.

I offer to clean up as soon as we're finished eating, and Denver puts together the stroller and gets Sammy situated. Plus, it gives me some time to think.

Not that the time helps.

The only thing I've figured out by the time we leave the house is I'm going to come out to him on this walk. I figure this has to be like a Band-Aid situation and just rip it off. If shit's going to hit the fan, it's better to find out sooner rather than later. There is no way I will be able to hide my new attraction to him for long. I know I'll slip up, and hiding this could make things worse.

"I'm glad we decided to go on this walk. I ate way too much and need to work it off," I state as I push the stroller, trying to fill the time with some light conversation.

"Same. I think I might lift some weights later," Denver remarks.

"Mind if I join you?"

Denver turns his head toward some birds flying by and shrugs. "Why not?" he replies, but he doesn't sound too thrilled.

Shit, is he picking up on the emotional storm I've been dealing with all morning?

"If you want to work out on your own, I don't mind. I don't want to bother you," I tell him.

He doesn't respond this time. His focus stays on the sky, and this weird wave of insecurity washes over me.

"You okay?" I question.

"I'm fine," he replies, but he still won't look at me.

Just up the way, I spot a bench and make a beeline for it. I sit down as soon as the stroller is pulled off the path. "I think we need to talk," I tell him.

This time, he turns to me, his gaze locking with mine.

"Why? I said I'm fine." He presses his lips together and grabs the back of his neck as he kicks at some rocks.

"Well, maybe I'm not," I respond, trying to keep my voice soft but failing.

His eyes go wide, and he swallows. My eyes are again drawn to how his Adam's apple bobs.

Why is that hot? And why does it make my heart race? Is that normal?

"Is something wrong?" he asks.

I pat the bench beside me, wanting him closer. He doesn't move at first, but he finally sits beside me after a few beats.

"Have you ever questioned your sexuality?" I ask, staring into the tree line.

The air is calm, so the leaves aren't rattling except when a bird or a squirrel disturbs a branch. It's a beautiful afternoon, and I'd be soaking it all in under normal circumstances.

Denver doesn't respond right away, and as much as I want to look at him, I'm scared I'll lose my gumption if I do.

Right when I'm about to continue, Denver speaks, his voice barely loud enough to hear. "I've questioned a lot of things in life." Deciding I need to be looking at my best friend, I turn and find scared gray eyes staring back at me. "Why are you asking?"

I take a second before responding, trying to find the right words. "Because I don't think I'm as straight as I once thought I was."

What looks like hopefulness replaces the fear on his face, and he licks his lips before responding. "What made you think that?"

I close my eyes as this flood of embarrassment takes over. I knew he would ask this question, but even though he's hinted at not being straight, I don't want to assume that means he's into me. This could still wreck our friendship.

"I had a dream about a man," I tell him as honestly as possible, opening my eyes to dare risk his expression.

His face is stoic, and I have a hard time figuring out what he's thinking. "And how did that make you feel?" he asks, his tone calm, steady.

"Confused, anxious, turned on… a bunch of things," I admit. "It's happened twice, actually. The second one, though, I didn't want it to be a dream."

"That all sounds normal. I remember the first time I developed feelings for a guy," he confesses, and my eyes damn near pop out of my head. Although there was a slight hint of him questioning his sexuality a moment ago, his words still throw me for a loop, but I don't know what to say. "I didn't have the balls like you do to bring it up to anyone. I kind of dealt with it on my own. Eventually, I asked some buddies at work, but that took a few months."

"Why didn't you come to me?" I ask, feeling a little bit offended. "Did you think I'd be an asshole or something?"

He shakes his head. "It's not as easy as that," he mutters. "I knew you'd be fine with me being bi. I wasn't so sure you'd be okay with me being into *you*."

His admission steals the air from my lungs, and I'm sure I look like a deer caught in the headlights right now. "See, that's how I thought you'd react," he says and looks away.

I quickly place my hand on his, which is resting on the bench beside me. His eyes dart to them, and his brows pull together, but he doesn't pull away.

"I'm not upset, idiot," I tell him, and his eyes finally meet mine again. "I'm just shocked because I'm into *you*."

"You... me... what?" he stammers, not forming a coherent sentence.

I chuckle and shrug. "I've been freaking out all morning about how to tell you because the last thing I wanted was to lose you. Hell, even making things awkward between us would be torture. I had no idea you were bi or into me. I thought this was all on me. I'll be honest... I'm not sure exactly what is going on, but you're my best friend, and I'm attracted to you. You already know I love you, but I think it's morphing into something more."

"When did you start feeling like this?" he asks, still looking confused.

He's trembling under my touch but doesn't move his hand.

"Honestly, I'm not one hundred percent positive. For sure yesterday, but I think it's been gradually happening over the last few weeks, possibly even longer."

"Maybe it's just the baby and the lack of sleep that's fucking with your head," he murmurs.

"When did you start having feelings for me?" I repeat his question to him, ignoring his perception of the situation because this doesn't feel like sleep deprivation. At first, maybe I was thinking the same thing, but there is something inside me screaming that's not what this is.

His eyes dart to the sky before they fall shut for a moment. "About a year ago," he whispers.

"You went that long dealing with this all on your own?" I hate that he felt like he couldn't come to me, but I understand why.

"Like I said, I asked the guys at work a few questions but didn't spill all the beans. I'm not sure why. You're who I turn to for shit like this. It wasn't exactly like I could say, 'Hey, we've been best friends since we were kids, but the night you accidentally sent me a dick pic woke something inside of me, and now, I can't stop thinking about you.' "

The night he's talking about pops into my head. Samantha and I were on shaky ground, and I was trying to spice things up. Except when I sent the picture, it went to Denver first. I was so fucking embarrassed, but he played it off like it was no big deal. Clearly, it meant more than he led me to believe.

What would have happened had he talked to me about it then? Would that have changed things between us? Would it have made me come to this bi-awakening sooner?

I know everything happens for a reason, and dwelling on what-ifs is a bad idea, but that doesn't stop them from popping up.

"That's why you started putting up a wall," I muse out loud, under my breath, finally connecting the dots.

"I didn't want my newfound feelings for you to affect our friend-ship," Denver whispers. "I was eventually going to tell you I'm bi, or pan, or not straight, but I wanted to wait until we weren't living together. I know you aren't homophobic, but this is something new and big, and you were already going through so much."

Denver's fingers twitch underneath mine, and it's then I realize my hand is still on his.

"I'm sorry you had to go through that alone," I tell him, squeezing his hand.

The corners of his lips turn up a bit, and his eyes lock onto mine. "I knew you'd have my back when I was ready to tell you. I just didn't know you'd start having the same feelings."

He flips his hand over so he can squeeze back, and this sudden feeling of rightness washes over me.

"What do you want to do about these feelings?" I question after the silence stretches for more than a few beats. When he doesn't respond, I take the opportunity to tell him how I feel. "I was thinking the other night about how perfect life feels with you by my side. I even thought if only you were a woman, I wouldn't have to look for anyone else. Now I realize you don't have to be a woman, and this could be what we've been wanting. I feel like I should be freaking out, but I'm not. I mean, I was, but only about how you would take this. Now that I know you feel the same way, that panic is set to rest. You've always been my constant, Denver. Why can't you be more than that?"

"You just found out you're not straight, and you already want to jump into a relationship? Don't you want some time to think about things? Maybe go to a gay bar and kiss a guy who isn't your best friend?" he asks.

I shake my head. "Why do I have to do that?"

Denver shrugs. "It's what I did."

The realization that he's more experienced with this than I am washes over me. "How many guys have you been with?" I question, hating how rude I sound. "I mean, if you want to tell me, that is."

"I've kissed a few guys and had a couple blow jobs but haven't gone farther than that," he tells me. "It was enough experimenting to figure out I wasn't straight, and it wasn't *just* you who did it for me, but at the same time, I wasn't into any of them enough to cross any more bridges."

"And you think I have to do the same experimenting?"

He shakes his head, staring at the sky. "I don't know," he whispers. "I guess I'm just scared about us jumping into this so quickly after you just started to figure these things out…" He pauses, taking a deep breath. "I don't want to lose this friendship. What if we try this, and it all goes south?" He finally looks back at me with brows pulled together and concern lurking behind those perfect eyes.

I get why he's thinking like this, but my gut is standing strong on this one, telling me that a relationship with Denver is a good idea. Since it's never led me astray, I don't doubt it for a second.

"What if it's everything we've ever wanted?" I counter. "Don't you wonder why our relationships have never worked out in the past? Maybe what we needed all along was right under our noses, and we were too blind to see it. The blinders are gone now, and I'd really like to give this a go. But if you're not ready, I understand."

Denver closes his eyes, his hand shaking once more in my grasp.

"What if we go slow?" I suggest. "I don't want to experiment with other guys. It's obvious to me I'm not straight, and I'm into you. But if you're scared, we don't have to rush into anything."

"I can do slow," he says after a beat.

My cheeks hurt from how big I'm smiling. With one more squeeze of his hand, I stand and pull him with me.

"Let's finish our walk. Afterward, maybe we can watch a movie while Sammy sleeps," I say.

Denver laughs, and I feel like I missed the punchline.

"We can *try* to watch a movie, but I have a strong suspicion we'll both fall asleep again and wake up cuddling."

"Wait... that really happened? I thought it was just a dream," I respond, shaking my head.

"It really happened, and it freaked me out because I thought your subconscious was thinking I was Samantha. I didn't want you to know how much I liked it, so I snuck out of there as fast as humanly possible."

It's my turn to laugh. "Well, now that we both have told our secrets, you won't have to run away this time. I'd like to wake with you in my arms and not think it's a dream this time."

The tips of his ears turn a pinkish red from his blush. I bet it's on his cheeks too, but his short beard is doing a good job covering it. "I'd like that too," he whispers, and we continue our walk.

One hand easily pushes the stroller while the other firmly holds Denver's. My heart does a funny little flip, and I realize it's been telling me how it feels about Denver all along, but I was pushing the feelings aside.

I won't be doing that anymore. I've always been someone who goes for the things I want, and I want Denver.

Chapter Seven

DENVER

"Queue up whatever you want to watch. I'll put Sammy down for his nap," Ford tells me as we walk into the house.

With quick feet, he starts to carry his son down the hall to the nursery when I call out after him. "Want me to make a bottle?"

He pauses, turning to beam at me. "That would be amazing, thank you," he says before disappearing into Sammy's room.

The few minutes alone gives me time to think while the Baby Barista makes the bottle. I'm still struggling to wrap my head around the bomb Ford dropped on me during our walk. Never in a million years did I imagine he'd develop feelings for me. And the fact he's dealing with it so much better than I did is even more confusing. Although Ford has always been the kind of guy to trust his gut, so honestly, I shouldn't be surprised.

Once the bottle is ready, I make my way to the nursery but stop in my tracks as I enter the room. Nothing crazy is happening. It's just Ford singing gently to Sammy, but my heart races like a speeding bullet. Watching my best friend with his son is something I could do all day long. Now I don't have to worry about getting caught staring. Yet part of me is still nervous about it.

I'm a lot more cautious than Ford is about things, so this is going to take me a while to get used to.

Ford lifts Sammy off the changing table and kisses his head, and it makes me want to swoon. There's just something about seeing a man care for a baby that is a massive turn-on.

Sammy screams, pulling me from my dirty thoughts. Gently, I rap on the door since Ford hasn't seen me yet.

"Bottle for the hungry man?" I singsong, and Ford offers me the best smile in return.

"Thank you so much. You're a lifesaver. Sammy did *not* want to cooperate with his diaper change and ended up needing a new outfit."

I chuckle. "It happens."

As I hand him the bottle, our fingers brush against each other, sending jolts of electricity through my veins. With how Ford's eyes go wide, I'm positive he felt it too.

After we lock eyes and stare at each other, Ford leisurely moves toward me. *Holy shit, is he going to kiss me?*

Sammy chooses that moment to cry again, and I'm thankful for the interruption. Now that the possibility is here, I'm not sure I am ready.

"I'll go get the movie queued up," I murmur, rushing out of the room.

As much as I wanted Ford to kiss me, I'm not sure now is the right time. We need to take things slow. I'm still wrapping my head around the fact that this is actually happening.

You'd think now that Ford has admitted to liking me more than just friends, the anxiety would all be washed away, but I swear it's gotten worse. Obviously, this is what I've been dreaming would happen, but I've also learned dreams are often better than reality.

A million what-ifs are playing in my head, making my stomach roll.

What if we try this, and it blows up in our faces?

What if Ford is simply sleep-deprived and ends up hating me for pushing this on him?

What if Ford changes his mind and takes Sammy away from me, leaving me all alone?

Once I'm in Ford's room, I grab the remote and search for a movie while pacing the room. Nothing is pulling my attention. All I can think about is that we're about to be in bed together for the first time as more than friends.

Knowing I need to talk to someone about all these garbled-up emotions inside me, I drop the remote on the bed and pull my phone out of my pocket, calling Nixon and praying he isn't busy.

"Aren't you supposed to be off today?" he answers gruffly.

I chuckle. "Can't I call for reasons outside of work? I thought we were friends," I tease.

He lets out a low belly laugh, and a tiny bit of my anxiety eases. "What's up?" he asks.

Just like that, all of the nervous energy returns tenfold.

"You know how a while ago I was asking questions about sexuality?"

"Sure do. You going to tell me the whole story now?"

An awkward laugh escapes my lips, and I grab the back of my neck.

"About a year ago, Ford accidentally sent me a dick pic," I begin, making Nixon laugh. "At first, I was shocked, but then I was turned on, and that quickly turned into panic. I was a mess, which is why I brought it up to you guys without *really* giving any details."

"So you were suddenly attracted to your best friend and didn't know what to do?"

I sigh. "Pretty much. The conversation at the bar with you and the other guys from work settled some of my nerves, but I still didn't know what to do. I thought maybe it was a one-time thing, so I started doing some experiments."

"Went to a gay bar?" Nixon guesses.

I chuckle because he hit the nail on the head. "Yup, and watched gay porn. I found out I had a preference, just like women, and that I definitely wasn't straight anymore. But just as I was coming to grips with my sexuality, Ford broke up with Samantha and needed a place to stay. My attraction grew into a full-blown crush, and I had no idea what I was supposed to do about it. I know you aren't supposed to fall for your straight best friend."

"You can't control who you have feelings for. Only how you act on them," Nixon states.

"I know that too, but I couldn't just cut him out of my life. Hell, I couldn't even push him aside because he needed me. I thought I could keep pushing my feelings down and that he'd move out one day, and I could move on."

"How's that working out for you?" Nixon asks.

I pause before responding, wondering how much I should say. I don't want to out Ford before he's ready, but I need advice here. And Nixon is good at keeping secrets. He won't tell a soul.

I take a deep breath, readying myself to tell him the new information I received today. "I was doing okay at keeping my secret to myself until Ford dropped a bomb on me today. Turns out, he's been having his own bi-awakening and wants to try being more than friends."

"Why don't you sound excited about that? Isn't that what you were hoping for?"

"I thought so, but now I'm even more anxious. He's had so much going on. What if it's just sleep deprivation, and he doesn't actually feel this way? I can't lose him, Nixon."

We're both silent for a minute, letting my confession sink in.

"You're both adults, and if Ford says he wants this, you have to trust him. I'm not a fortune teller and can't predict how this will turn out, but do you want to stop it now because of the possibility it will fail?"

"I don't know," I whisper.

"Well, you have to figure that out. If you need me, I'm here, but this is something you have to decide for yourself. What I do want you to keep in mind, though, is how much you want fear to hold you back. Sometimes we have to throw caution to the wind and go for what we want, even if it scares the shit out of us."

I take a deep breath, staring at the ceiling and letting his words sink in.

"Thanks for your help. I'll keep that all in mind," I tell him.

We say quick goodbyes, and I end the call before picking the remote back up to try to find anything to watch. Unable to sit still, I resume my pacing as I do so.

"Find anything good?" Ford asks from the doorway while I'm still scrolling through Netflix.

"Not really. But I heard this new baking show was funny. It also wouldn't be the end of the world if we passed out while watching it," I joke.

Ford chuckles and sits on the bed. I don't move right away, and he lifts a brow at me as if to say *Are you joining me?* After a deep breath, I follow suit, joining him, but the anxious energy doesn't leave my body.

"You gonna put the show on?" he asks, brows pulled slightly together, obviously trying to figure out what's going on with me.

I nod and hit the button on the remote. The episode starts, yet I can't help but fidget. An awkward air takes over the room as we sit beside each other and try to watch the show.

"Are you okay?" Ford asks after a few minutes, picking up on the tension radiating off me.

I turn to stare into his eyes I so often get lost in. "I'm scared," I confess quietly.

"I'll admit I'm a little nervous too."

"That makes sense. This is all new to you."

"Why are you scared?" he asks with soft eyes that make me want to spill everything.

"I don't want to lose you," I admit. "I also don't understand how you're accepting all of this so fast. When I started developing feelings for you, I freaked out. The fact that you aren't is making my head reel."

The corners of his lips tip up, lighting his face in a way I've grown to love.

"Well, I did freak out, but not about my sexuality or wanting to be with you. I also don't want to lose you. You're my best friend, and I don't want to live in a world without you by my side. If you only wanted to be friends, I would live with that, but if you want more, I'm here."

"It's really that simple to you, isn't it?"

He shrugs. "You know me, I trust my intuition and run with it. But that doesn't mean I'm not anxious as well. I just came to the realization that I'm not straight this morning. The idea of being with you feels right, but starting anything is risky as fuck."

I nod but don't speak. I'm not sure what to say.

"But I believe the reward is worth the risk," he adds. "Besides, if you think about *everything* we've been through, there isn't even a real risk. It will be awkward at first if things don't work out between us, and that would suck, but we'll get through it and still be friends. It's how we've always been. There is no way we'd let anything come between our friendship."

The way he's coming across so sure settles some of my nerves.

"You make it sound easy," I murmur.

He chuckles and grabs my hand, staring into my eyes intently. "It isn't going to be easy, but whatever life has thrown at us, we've always come out the other side as a team. This isn't going to be any different."

His words are like a calming balm on my nerves. *Is this actually happening?*

"How have you not had more girlfriends? You clearly have a way with words," I joke, trying to break the tension.

Ford laughs. "Maybe there was a reason for that."

Ford is taking this all in stride, and it's a little surreal. While his ease about everything is gradually setting my mind at rest, I feel like someone needs to pinch me.

We turn our attention toward the show, and while a bit of tension is still filling the small space, it also feels natural. That's probably because, even though things are changing between us, our friendship is still a solid foundation.

"Could I hold you?" Ford whispers as a contestant puts a cake in the oven.

I nod, not trusting my voice. Ford adjusts himself so he's lying down with his back and head propped up slightly on a few pillows, then he opens his arms for me. Tentatively, I move so my head is resting on his chest, and he wraps his strong arms around me. Once we're settled, I let out a breath I wasn't aware I was holding.

Holy shit. I'm cuddling with my best friend. I can't believe this is happening.

"You fit perfectly in my arms," he notes.

A smile creeps across my face, but again, I don't respond.

Honestly, I'm not sure what to say. He's right. This feels perfect.

Little by little, all the anxiety I was harboring lessens. Everything feels like it's falling into place too easily, and it terrifies me. I keep wondering when something crazy is going to happen.

It can't be this simple, can it?

Chapter Eight

FORD

WHILE DENVER SWEEPS THE kitchen, I'm feeding Sammy with a smile on my face. Apparently, I didn't do the *best* job at cleaning up after breakfast.

Can you blame me, though? I was a bit distracted.

Thankfully, Sammy had a decent nap this afternoon, and it meant Denver and I also had a decent rest. Who knew holding my best friend would result in the best sleep I've had in the longest time?

"Would you like to go on a date tonight?" I ask randomly.

The question clearly throws Denver off his axis. His eyes go wide briefly before he cools his expression. I know he's still getting used to the fact I feel the same way about him that he does about me. To be honest, *I'm* still getting used to it, but even though I'm a bit anxious, I still want to give this my all. Denver doesn't deserve to be treated like a dirty little secret.

It's still a mind fuck that only yesterday I thought I was straight, and now that label doesn't fit me anymore, yet deep down, I know this is right. My gut is one hundred percent on board with wanting to be in a relationship with Denver. Now I just need to prove it to him.

A simple date is moving slow, right?

"What did you have in mind?" he questions, leaning on the broom.

"Well, it will have to be somewhere kid-friendly as we have a third wheel for this date," I state as Sammy spits out the bottle, and I adjust him on my shoulder to burp him.

Denver beams at me. "The only acceptable third wheel for a first date."

"How 'bout I do a little research. I'll plan something extra special."

Denver's chest rises and falls as he takes a deep breath and slowly blows it out, causing me to wiggle a little in the chair. *Maybe a date isn't slow enough for him, but how much slower does he expect us to go?*

"I think I can work with that," he finally responds.

The anxiety creeping its way up my veins releases, along with the squeezing sensation in my chest.

Sammy chooses that moment to let out a large burp, and we both laugh. But my laugh quickly turns to a gag as a loud gurgling sound comes from his pants.

"Want to take this one?" I ask as a shudder works its way up my spine, and I gag again. *Why can't I handle shit?*

Denver laughs at me, but like a knight in shining armor, he sets the broom to rest against the counter and makes his way over to us.

"You're lucky you're hot as fuck," he murmurs, grabbing Sammy from me. "I wouldn't change this many diapers for just anyone."

I blow him a kiss as he walks away, then call out, "You're the best."

His laughter reverberates down the hall, and a giant grin is firmly planted on my lips.

Knowing the diaper change will take at least a few minutes, I grab my phone from the end table and search for tonight's ideas.

This date has to be perfect. I need to show Denver how I'm feeling.

An ad for a special stargazing event at the planetarium tonight pops up during my search, which grabs my attention. I read through the details and decide it's perfect. Once I've confirmed everything is correct, I download the digital tickets and make my way to the nursery, where Denver is humming to Sammy.

"You're a better singer than I am," I whisper, trying not to startle him.

"Obviously," he jokes as he looks over his shoulder and winks at me.

"I've got the date planned," I tell him, moving to the changing table and running my fingers gently over Sammy's head and through the soft wisps of his baby hair.

"Do I get to know what it is, or is it a surprise?" Denver asks as he slides Sammy's pants on and picks him up.

"Surprise," I reply, beaming at him. "We need to leave the house right after dinner, though."

Denver stares at me as if he's trying to read my mind and figure out the details of what I have up my sleeve, but then he shrugs. "How should I dress?" he asks.

Suddenly, the image of him without any clothes pops into my head, and my mouth goes dry. Clearing my throat, I push the thought aside and try to figure out how to talk again.

"However you want," I manage to get out, though my voice is hoarse.

I'm met with a raised brow on a handsome face, but thankfully, he doesn't push to ask what just happened. We're supposed to be taking it slow, so I probably shouldn't be picturing him naked. But I'm only fucking human, and his question sent my brain straight into the gutter.

"How do you think Sammy will take being out of the house past his normal bedtime?" Denver asks, moving past me to head toward the living room.

"He doesn't really sleep as it is, and he likes to be in his car seat more than his bed anyway," I respond with a shrug. "We might actually have a better evening this way."

"That actually makes sense," Denver states, lowering himself to his knees next to Sammy's play mat and putting Little Man on his tummy.

I sit next to him and smile at my son.

"I know it's only been a day since we've started him on the medication, but hopefully, it doesn't take long to start, and he sleeps better in his bed," I add while Sammy pushes to lift his head and chest. I'm in awe of how strong he is.

Denver nods. "Fingers crossed."

Sammy plays on his tummy for a while, and I help Denver with dinner. Since we ate a later breakfast, we skipped lunch, needing sleep more than food. And early works well for my plans tonight.

"The cheese should only take five minutes to melt," Denver states as he puts the casserole in the oven.

"Perfect, I'll give Sammy a quick diaper change so he isn't upset while we eat," I supply as I make my way to my son, who is starting to fuss.

"Come on, handsome, let's get you a dry bum," I coo at him while heading for the nursery.

Once he is clean and dry, I carry him to the kitchen and place him in his vibrating chair while Denver dishes up our plates.

"This smells so good," I praise as Denver puts the plates on the table and sits beside me.

A small moan leaves my lips as the aroma wafts around me, and Denver chuckles in response. "You know, noises like that are supposed to be reserved for the bedroom," he teases with a waggle of his brows.

Heat creeps up my cheeks, and I'm sure my face is the color of a tomato as my thoughts travel into the gutter once again. "My bedroom noises are different," I respond with what I'm hoping is a flirtatious smile. "Maybe you'll be able to compare the two later." I wink, earning me a tiny gasp from Denver's plump lips.

My eyes zero in on his mouth as his tongue darts out to wet his lips. *Fuck, I want to kiss him so badly, but I also promised to take this slow. Would that be crossing a line?*

My stomach gurgles, breaking me from my thoughts, and I force out a laugh. "I guess I'm hungrier than I thought," I murmur, turning my attention to the plate in front of me.

We keep the conversation light as we eat, but I wonder if Denver is as nervous as I am. Not because I'm about to go on a date with a man but because I'm going on a date with my best friend. I want to do this, but I'm terrified I'm going to mess it up.

Samantha used to complain that I wasn't very romantic. I struggled with wooing her when she would whine about the romance dying.

What if that happens with Denver?

What if I just suck at being a boyfriend?

"Are you okay?" Denver asks as he grabs my now empty plate and takes it to the sink.

"Just nervous," I admit instead of playing it off like it's no big deal.

"Me too," he whispers.

"Well, I'm glad I'm not the only one. I want tonight to be special, but I'm scared I'm going to fuck it up."

Denver chuckles and opens his arms for me. I don't hesitate before stepping in and squeezing him tightly.

"Let's stop acting like we've never been out together before. Yes, this is different, but there is no way you're going to fuck it up," he tells me as he holds me.

Some of my worries float away, but as soon as I step away, I miss his embrace.

"I'm going to get myself and Sammy ready. Let's meet by the front door in thirty minutes," I suggest.

"Sounds like a plan," he replies as I make my way over to Sammy.

"Ready to go on a special outing?" I ask, lifting him.

He smacks his lips at me in response, which means he's getting hungry. If things go according to plan, he'll eat before we leave and sleep most of the date. I make a mental note to pack an extra bottle just in case.

As I'm getting ready, my heart beats a mile a minute.

I'm about to go on a date with my best friend.

Holy shit.

Chapter Nine

DENVER

AFTER FORD PULLS INTO the parking lot of the planetarium, I shoot him a funny look. "Isn't this where schools take kids to learn about space?"

"It's for everyone," Ford tells me with a smirk.

God, he must think I'm an idiot.

"Well, I know that," I respond dryly. "I've just never known adults to hang out here."

"There's a first time for everything, right?"

I nod, and we both get out of the car. Since Sammy's car seat is installed on my side, I pull him out, and my heart melts a little to see him already sleeping peacefully. His thick lips are puckered into the world's cutest pout, and his light lashes lie softly against his upper cheek. He's perfect.

"Are you sure this place is stroller-friendly?" I ask as Ford unfolds the stroller.

"Yu*p*!" He pops the *p* on the word, and I can't help but chuckle. "I triple-checked. I also sent an email to make sure we could bring Sammy to this event. I was assured he'd be more than welcome."

It shouldn't surprise me how prepared Ford is. It's one of his key personality traits. Yet it still warms my heart that he thought of everything.

Once the stroller is ready, I click Sammy's carrier into it and walk side by side with Ford into the planetarium.

"Wow," I whisper as we enter.

Hanging from the entryway's ceiling is an entire mechanical solar system. Plants move around, and stars twinkle. The lights are dimmed currently, making it even more breathtaking.

"This place is actually super cool," I tell Ford, who has a giant grin plastered on his face.

"I spent a good amount of time checking out their website. I couldn't wait to actually be here in person. Just wait until we get to the good part." He winks, placing his hand on top of mine so we can push the stroller together.

The sudden action causes my heart rate to pick up. It's becoming more real that I'm on a date with my best friend right now.

"Come on," Ford says with a tilt of his head, guiding us to a different part of the building.

"Do you have tickets?" a lady asks.

Ford smiles and pulls out his phone to show her the digital tickets.

"Excellent. You can take the elevator right behind me to the second floor. Then you'll follow the hall to the end to the dome theater where the Love Under the Stars event is taking place," she instructs.

At the lady's words, I shoot Ford a questioning glance, but he simply shrugs before pushing the stroller, forcing me to move or let go. Considering how much I'm enjoying his touch, I walk along with him.

"Love Under the Stars, huh?" I tease once we're in the elevator, making Ford blush.

"It's supposed to be romantic. We each get one glass of wine with our ticket price and will be able to spend two hours learning about the stars and planets. It's designed for couples, so there won't be too many teenagers or crazy kids running around."

"Just a cute baby sleeping," I add.

Ford chuckles. "I'm praying he doesn't cause too much of a fuss. I'd hate to ruin people's night."

"I'm sure he'll be fine. If he causes a fuss during any of the presentations, we'll just excuse ourselves for a moment," I state, and Ford's smile grows even wider.

"You're already the perfect boyfriend," he tells me before leaning in for a kiss on my cheek.

A tingly sensation takes over my body, yet at the same time, a sudden rush of panic runs through my veins. *This is fucking happening,* I think, and I don't know what to do about it. The elevator dings right then, saving me from my crazy thoughts.

We exit and follow the instructions of the nice lady toward where we need to be.

"Here for the Love Under the Stars event?" a man in a purple shirt, the same as the lady downstairs, asks, and we nod. "Excellent, right this way." He points us in the right direction. "You can get your glass of wine now. The first presentation will be starting shortly."

We thank him and grab a glass of white from a table behind him.

For first dates, I have to hand it to Ford. This is pretty fucking special. It's also kind of nice being on the receiving end of the planning. Although the wheels in my brain are spinning to figure out what I could do to top this for our next date.

I'm still nervous about trying this with Ford, but there's no way I can stop it. I have to trust that our friendship is solid enough to handle anything we throw at it.

With wine in hand, Ford and I mosey about to check out the items on display. Any time we pause, our hands interlock. I'm not even sure if either of us is conscious that we're doing it. It's almost as if it's a natural thing to happen.

And I kind of love it.

This might be the best date of my life, and it's not because of what we're doing but who I'm with.

"Who's a hungry little man?" Ford asks Sammy when we walk into the house after the best date of my life. Even when Sammy started fussing toward the end of the night, it didn't put a damper on things.

Speaking of the devil, Sammy makes a noise that we interpret as *I am. Please feed me.*

"I'll get him changed and swaddled if you get the bottle ready," I suggest.

The way Ford's face lights up in response makes my heart beat a little faster.

"Thank you," he whispers.

"Well, I need to hold onto the title of best boyfriend," I tease with a wink before heading down the hall to the nursery.

Sammy wiggles and squawks while I change his wet diaper and get him into a pair of soft footie pajamas.

"The bottle is coming, Little Man," I assure him when he starts to fuss a little more.

Thankfully, Ford walks in at that exact moment like a genie granting a wish.

"Would you like to feed him?" I ask after I finish the swaddle.

"Yes, please. I love the bonding moments of a feed. Even if that means I don't sleep as well."

"I was thinking it might be better if I take on more of the nighttime feeds since you're going back to work in two days," I state.

With my job, I have the luxury of working from home if needed. Ford doesn't.

Before Sammy, Ford would work long hours on typical cases. Seeing as they are making him go back two weeks earlier than planned for a specific one makes me think things will be even more hectic than normal.

If things weren't insane, they wouldn't be calling him. They'd let him have his scheduled days off and let him spend more time with his son.

"You don't have to do that," Ford protests. I lift a brow at him, and he sighs. "We'll figure it out, but if I'm on a day off, I'm taking the night feeds."

"Deal," I say with laughter, handing Sammy off.

Once he is safely in his father's arms, I head to the kitchen, allowing the two of them to have their moment, and get to work making us a snack while I wait for Ford to finish with Sammy.

I'm lost in thought when Ford comes out and announces, "He's asleep."

My timer goes off right then, and I smile at him. "Hungry?" I ask, moving toward the oven to pull out the nachos.

"I wasn't, but those smell so good," he states, leaning against the island.

"Why don't you put on a show in the living room? We can snack and relax there," I suggest as I grab plates.

"Sounds like a plan," he replies, turning on his heels.

The tone of the streaming service firing up fills the quiet space, and it doesn't take me long to join him with food in hand.

"Thanks for the perfect first date," I tell him as I sit next to him.

"It was nothing," he responds with a big grin.

"So now that we're officially dating, how do we want to handle this?" I ask after some time passes. "Are we keeping this to ourselves or letting everyone know?"

"You're not a dirty secret, Denver. We'll do this like we've done in any relationship. Tell the people closest to us that we're together, and everyone else will eventually find out. We can tell your mom when she comes down next weekend."

"Yeah, that's probably best to be done in person. What about inviting some of our friends over for a game night and telling them then?"

"That's a good idea. Maybe I'll call Samantha first thing in the morning and let her know. She doesn't deserve to find out from anyone else. And Mary is coming over for a visit tomorrow afternoon, so it's best if we get that out of the way sooner rather than later," Ford states.

"How do you think Samantha's going to handle it?" I question as my stomach rumbles with nerves.

Ford seems to pick up on my anxious energy and runs his hand up and down my spine, calming me in no time.

"Honestly, I think she's going to be fine with it. She used to joke about you and me being perfect for each other all the time. She'll probably say it makes perfect sense."

He isn't wrong. I wonder if she saw things we missed.

We eat our nachos in comfortable silence while the show plays. Once my plate is empty, a big yawn escapes my lips.

"I guess it's time for bed," I murmur before yawning again.

"Would you like to sleep in my bed tonight?" Ford asks, catching me slightly off guard. "I really enjoyed holding you while we napped this afternoon."

The way he nibbles on his lip and his brows pull together has me refusing to say no.

"I'd like that," I respond, and Ford's smile grows impossibly large.

Standing, I collect our plates and place them in the kitchen before following Ford to bed.

"Do you want me to wear pajamas?" he asks.

I can't help but laugh. "Why would I want that?"

Ford shrugs. "I promised we'd take this slow. I want to make sure you're comfortable."

Stepping forward, I wrap my arms around his neck, staring deeply into his eyes. "I'm still nervous, but this feels right. Your being open with your communication is helping calm me. So no, you don't have to wear pajamas. Boxers are fine."

He chuckles and places his hands on my hips, giving me a tug into him.

A gasp leaves my mouth right before my best friend's lips land on mine. Fireworks dance behind my eyelids as I melt into him. I've never had a better kiss in my entire life. A little moan breaks free as Ford's tongue licks at the seam of my lips. I open for him, allowing him to deepen the kiss.

"You're an amazing kisser," I whisper after we break for air.

"That was the best kiss of my life," he confesses, filling my chest with pride.

Right then, another big yawn slips past my lips. Even the need coursing through my veins can't push aside how absolutely exhausted I am.

"As much as I'd like to have another kiss like that, I think sleep is in order," I mutter.

Ford nods, also yawning. "We'll have more time for kissing tomorrow."

I can't help but laugh as we both shuck our clothes and climb into bed together. The only barrier between us is the thin material of our boxers.

Ford checks the monitor before settling into bed and cuddling me from behind. "Thanks for going out with me tonight," he whispers, pulling me in closer.

His hairy chest rubs against my back, and his erection presses firmly into my ass. If we didn't need sleep so desperately, I'd say fuck going slow and grind against him, but I can barely keep my eyes open.

Sleep is the smarter decision.

"Thanks for asking me out," I respond quietly.

Soft lips press against my shoulder before we both relax into the mattress, letting sleep pull us under.

Chapter Ten

FORD

"Hey, handsome, long time no talk. What's up?" Samantha answers, which makes the knot in my stomach tighten.

Last night was the best night of my life, but I've been dreading this call since I woke up. Denver is currently cooking us breakfast while Sammy has some tummy time on his play mat.

For the last ten minutes, I've been pacing the bedroom floor, trying to work up the courage to make this call. I'm nervous because the last thing I want to do is hurt Samantha. I think she'll be happy for us, but what if I'm wrong?

"A lot, actually... got a minute to talk?" I spit out.

"For you? Of course," she replies.

My heart races as I try to think of what to say next. "Are you ready for the big move?" I ask, not wanting to drop the bomb right out of the gate.

"Almost. I still can't believe this is actually happening. In less than one week, I'll finally be in Miami, living my dream." She lets out a little squeal, and her happiness warms my heart. "Speaking of living the dream... how's Sammy doing?"

"Growing like a weed. Still not sleeping the best, but we have him on acid reflux medication, so hopefully things will be changing for the better soon."

"Oh, that's good. I can't imagine how it would be to have a baby who cries all the time. Fingers crossed, the meds work. Mom told me she's coming over for a visit this afternoon."

I take a deep breath and decide now would be the perfect time to tell her about Denver.

"She is... that's one of the reasons I was calling..." I take a breath, trying to figure out how best to tell her what's going on. "I went on a date last night," I blurt out, and the line goes silent, making me wonder if the call dropped. "Are you still there?"

"Yeah, sorry. Shit." She pauses. "I guess I just didn't see this coming so soon."

"To be honest, me neither. It kind of just happened."

"I'm happy for you, Ford. How did you meet her? I thought you were spending most of your time at home with Denver."

"About that... it's actually Denver I went out with." Again, I'm met with silence.

"Are you shitting me right now?" she says.

"Not at all. My feelings for him are brand new, but it feels right, so I didn't want to fight it."

All of a sudden, laughter fills my ear. I'm not sure what I was expecting, but it wasn't that.

"Shit..." She gasps for air between bouts of laughter. "I feel like I should have seen this coming. God, this makes so much sense."

"Well, you're the only one who thinks that. Both Denver and I are still wrapping our heads around this, but I guess he fell for me first."

"I thought something felt different between you two during the pregnancy. Are you sure this hasn't been going on for a while?"

"I just figured out I'm not straight yesterday, so pretty sure this is brand new."

She giggles. "Maybe I was picking up on Denver's feelings."

My heart flips with joy.

"I'm happy for you, Ford. If I had known you were bi, I would have suggested you two hook up a long time ago."

I can't help but laugh. "What about us?" I feign outrage.

"We were never meant to be forever. I would have let you go sooner had I known your soulmate was waiting for you."

"Hey, we just started this thing, so don't go throwing around words like that so soon," I chastise.

She laughs again, and I'm thankful this is going so well. The tight ball of nerves residing in my stomach before I made the call finally loosens.

"Do you think your mom is going to be okay with Denver and me dating?" I ask, the thought randomly popping into my head.

"I think so, but if she gives you shit, just let me know. I'll straighten her out," she promises, and again, I laugh. "Could you do me a favor while my mom is there, though?"

"Anything."

"If she brings up my move and tries to get you to convince me to stay, can you squash it? She's been giving me such a hard time. It would be nice to have someone else on my side. I know she's nervous about me being so far away, but this is what I've always wanted."

"I'll do my best, but your mom has always been stubborn," I point out.

She sighs. "I know, it's the worst. Good thing I'm not stubborn at all," she jokes, and I laugh so hard my sides hurt.

"I'm glad we're still friends," I tell her.

"Me too. Honestly, I think that's what we were meant to be all along. We were only fighting destiny."

We talk for a little bit longer, catching up on life before saying our goodbyes and hanging up. By the time I come out of my bedroom,

Denver is sitting on the floor next to Sammy, and a realization of how perfect this is washes over me.

What would life be like now if we had figured out our feelings for each other sooner? I shake my head because if that had happened, Sammy might not be here today, and I wouldn't want that. Everything happens for a reason.

"How did the call go?" Denver asks, snapping me from my daydream.

"Really good. She's happy for us," I tell him, then Sammy babbles. "He seems to be enjoying tummy time."

"I read that it helps with the acid in their bellies," he supplies, and I walk over to join them, sitting on the floor next to Denver.

"Makes sense. I'm glad he doesn't hate it. I've read a lot of baby books about the importance of tummy time."

"Same," Denver agrees.

"I love that you jumped headfirst into this with me, even when you were battling your internal feelings."

Denver shrugs. "It's what friends do. I'm still nervous about if this is really a good idea," he confesses quietly.

"Why wouldn't it be?" I question.

"I don't know. I've always sucked at relationships, and the only reason you and Samantha lasted so long was because you were comfortable. It wasn't because you were actually meant to be together. What if the same thing happens to us?"

He has a point, but I don't see it the same way.

"How about we agree to keep talking?" I suggest. "That was one of my biggest mistakes with Samantha. Maybe we would have ended it sooner if we were honest with each other."

Denver sighs but nods. "Okay. I'll try, but you know me, I suck at talking."

I chuckle. "That's an understatement, but you've always talked to me. We're adding a new layer to our relationship, but that shouldn't change our underlying foundation. We're best friends for a reason. We know each other better than anyone else."

Denver doesn't say anything, but words aren't needed right now. Leaning in, I press my lips to his. A small gasp escapes him, and I take the opportunity to deepen the kiss. My tongue slips in, dancing with his. Need curls around my spine and slithers through my veins.

Kissing Denver is like nothing I've ever experienced, and it's not just that he's the first man I've kissed. Although that is different, for sure. What hits me the hardest is this rush of contentment. Everyone I've kissed in the past felt great, but it didn't feel this life-changing. It's like my heart is screaming that it's finally found our person.

I roam my hand up and down Denver's side. His body is hard, muscular, and well-defined, with no soft curves like the women I've been with. He feels so right under my palms, and I love it. My dick comes to life, pushing against the restraint of my clothing. I need more, but just as I'm about to shove him to the floor, my stomach growls, killing the moment.

"Breakfast is keeping warm in the oven. Why don't we eat?" Denver suggests, and I pout in response, making him laugh. "We'll have time for exploring later."

My stomach rumbles again, and I groan. "Fine. Let's eat."

"How are you feeling about everything?" Denver asks as we sit at the table to eat our pancakes.

"Really good," I reply with a cheeky grin.

"Not freaking out? This is a lot newer to you than it is to me," he reminds me.

I place my hand on his thigh and squeeze it gently.

"I'm not freaking out," I assure him. "I feel like I'm exactly where I'm supposed to be right now, with the person meant for me. Nothing has ever felt this right."

Denver sucks in a breath and stares at his food before looking back at me and slowly blowing it out. His gray eyes shimmer with something, but it's not a look I recognize.

"Are *you* freaking out? Do we need to take a step back?" I check, worried that I'm pushing him farther than he's comfortable with.

He shakes his head. "I'm definitely caught up in a lot of emotions right now, but I don't want to take a step back. Cuddling with you last night and the two kisses we shared were fucking perfect. I'd really like to do more," he whispers.

My cock hardens in my sweats, and I let out a low growl before licking my lips. If it wasn't for my son sitting beside us, I'd be pulling my best friend into my lap.

Clearly feeling left out, Sammy lets out a squawk, pulling Denver and me from a heated staring contest.

"Are you hungry?" I ask my son, who lets out another little cry.

I pick him up off the floor, and a whiff of the reason Sammy turned fussy hits my nose, and I have to fight back a gag.

"Want to take this one?" I question, moving my son toward my best friend.

Or would boyfriend be the better word now?

The acidic scent must hit his nose then since he jerks his head back, furrowing his brows and scrunching his nose. He shakes his head, his eyes watering. "No can do. I've got to clean up. This poo-nami is all on you," he teases, standing and clearing the table.

"Come on, stinky boy, let's get this over with," I grumble and make my way to the nursery.

Denver's laughter follows me, and even though I know I'm going to gag this entire diaper change, I'm also smiling so wide my face hurts.

"Oh... my... God!" I gag when I pull Sammy's pants down.

His onesie is soaked in shit, and the smell is so bad it makes me lightheaded.

Don't pass out.

Taking a deep breath through my mouth, I hold it as I strip Sammy of his shitty clothes and throw them right in the trash. There is no way I'm going to try and get that out in the wash.

So long Super Baby onesie, you will be missed.

Once my son is naked, I decide the easiest form of action here will be a bath. It would probably take at least one hundred baby wipes to clean him. Even then, I wouldn't be satisfied he was clean enough.

I pick Sammy up in a way that supports his neck but also assures I'm not touching any of the mess covering his skin and rush to the bathroom. Using the shower head, I rinse the poop off my son, which he does not like one bit. His high-pitched cries tell me exactly how pissed off he is.

"Almost done," I assure him, but he doesn't stop screaming.

It doesn't take long for me to rinse him off and set him down in his baby bathtub. Thankfully, once the warm water starts to fill the tub, the crying settles, and Sammy seems happy again.

"See... I told you I wasn't a bad guy," I coo at him.

He splashes at the water, bringing a smile to my lips.

"Was it really that bad?" Denver asks, leaning against the door frame.

I glare at him. "I've never seen so much shit in my life," I deadpan, which makes him burst out laughing.

"Glad I got out of that one, then."

I can't help but chuckle as I shake my head.

"Is the kitchen clean?" I ask.

He nods and steps into the bathroom. His eyes trail down my body, obviously checking me out, but when they land on my chest, his nose scrunches and his lips press together in a firm line.

"Why don't I finish up here? You can get changed," he suggests, throwing me off a little, so I look down at my shirt and gag again.

"Fuck. I thought I was getting out of this unscathed," I holler, staring at a shit stain on my favorite white shirt. "Well, this is going in the garbage."

"We could probably get the stain out," Denver supplies, but I shake my head.

"Not worth the headache. I'll be back in a minute." I stand and make my way to my room.

I knew babies were gross, but this is a whole other level. I honestly never thought I was going to get shit on. I guess that was my mistake.

I'm careful as I remove the soiled article of clothing and shove it in the bathroom trash can.

Right as I'm straightening my clean T-shirt, my phone rings, and I see Melody's name on the screen.

"What's up?" I ask, moving to sit on my bed.

"Shit is getting crazy," she informs me with a sigh.

"What's happening now?"

"Heather Anderson's body was found just after you went on paternity leave," she starts, mentioning the case of a missing girl we were working on before I left.

We had been turning over every rock we could possibly find, trying to bring the girl home, but every lead led to a dead end. It was turning into a cold case, and I was beyond frustrated.

"And the coroner has discovered some disturbing news. It's why I need you back. This case is bigger than we thought."

"Fuck," I mutter, my blood rushing with anger. "I promise I'll be there on Monday. If anything else comes up in the meantime, please let me know."

"I will. I just wanted to fill you in a bit and let you know I'm not calling you in for no reason."

"I know you wouldn't do that," I reply.

Melody sighs, and I can feel how much this is weighing on her.

"I don't blame you for calling me back early. It sucks, but it isn't your fault."

"Thanks," she murmurs. "I kind of needed to hear that. I guess I'll see you on Monday."

"That you will," I say, then end the call.

By the time I get off the phone, Denver and Sammy are in the nursery.

"Who's all clean?" I coo at Sammy.

"He seems happy but tired, which is kind of perfect. If he naps now, he'll be up just in time for Mary to arrive," Denver supplies.

In a few long strides, I make my way to the changing table and pick up my son, who is finally all clean and fully dressed.

"Who do you want to give you your bottle?" I coo at Sammy. "Daddy or..." I pause, not sure what title Denver wants. "What do you want to be called?"

A look of insecurity washes over his face. "Um... I'm not sure. We just started dating, so anything other than uncle feels too soon," he supplies, and I shrug.

"It's not like he's exactly talking yet," I remind Denver, then turn my attention back to Sammy. "Who do you want to give you your bottle?" I ask again. "Daddy or Uncle D?"

"Uncle D? Really?"

"That's what happens when you don't come up with a proper response," I state. "But to be honest, I think papa would suit you better," I whisper as I pass him and make my way to the kitchen to prepare a bottle.

You'd think it would be weird to want to use that title so soon as Denver mentioned, but he's been in this since the beginning, and it feels right. If you take DNA out of the equation, he's just as much Sammy's dad as I am.

Chapter Eleven

DENVER

Papa.

The title lingers, nestling its way into my heart. How is it possible that one word has the ability to freeze me completely? So many emotions are dancing inside my head, and I don't know which one to cling to. The fear is one I'm used to, but this overwhelming joy is almost too much. It's like it intensifies the fear and anxiety, leaving me in a weird kind of fucked-up loop.

Forcing my feet to move, I follow Ford into the kitchen, where he already has the Baby Barista making up a bottle.

"Why don't you feed him?" I suggest. "I'll get some meal prep for lunch started."

"Excellent plan. Are you still making your famous potato salad?" he asks.

I nod. "That's the plan."

"Perfect, I can't wait," he says as the bottle finishes.

Once he's back in the nursery with Sammy, I work on what I need to do.

"Need any help?" Ford asks once he's back.

"I'm good, but thanks for the offer."

He smiles, makes his way over to me, and kisses my cheek.

"Any time," he whispers, then leans against the counter.

Things between us are progressing nicely. I'm so fucking happy it hurts, but I can't seem to push my insecurities and doubt entirely out of the way. Maybe if Ford was freaking out more, it would put me more at ease.

When I discovered I was bi, I lost my mind, but Ford is jumping right in. Maybe this would be easier to accept if I could trust my gut like Ford. The man doesn't let anything hold him back. When something feels right to him, he doesn't allow his mind to try to convince him otherwise. I've always envied that personality trait of his.

I'm a logical kind of guy. I need to weigh the pros and cons of something before heading in. I hate being blindsided, so it's almost impossible for me to commit if my ducks aren't all in a row.

Maybe that's what's happening right now. I don't feel like I have all the information needed to feel confident in our decision. But what more do I need?

I shake my head and move to the sink to drain the potatoes.

Somehow, Ford picks up on my stressful thoughts and rests his hand on my shoulder. "What's wrong?"

I sigh. "I'm trying to be as cool with this as you are, but it's like my brain is putting a block up. I don't know how to clear it."

"You don't feel like you have all the pieces to the puzzle, do you?" he guesses, once again proving how well he gets me.

"I think that's it, but I don't know what's missing," I grumble.

Ford squeezes my shoulder. "Can I tell you what I know?"

I nod and wait for him to continue.

"I know that we've been best friends since the moment we met as toddlers. I know that nobody knows me better than you do. I *know* that even though this is new territory for us, this is where we are meant to be. It's scary and exciting at the same time, but we're perfect for each other. Some may say I should be panicking right now, but how can I be scared when the person who's always had my back is standing by my side? You don't have anything to be afraid of because I'll never hurt you. Even if we don't work out as partners, nothing will break the friendship we have."

His words soothe the anxiety inside me, and finally, it's like I have some clarity. It only took my best friend almost smashing it into my head, but the weight that has been suffocating me is lifting.

Ford isn't accepting this easily because he doesn't know what he's doing. It's almost the opposite. He's not freaking out because, like he said, we're perfect for each other. Ford has never once lied to me, so if he says we'll be friends no matter what, I have to believe him.

Taking a deep inhale, I offer the man in front of me a small smile.

"You've definitely got a way with words," I tell him.

He chuckles. "So, are we good now?" he questions, his hand still on my shoulder.

I nod before throwing caution to the wind and leaning in for a simple kiss. Ford's tongue darts out right away to lick the seam of my lips, and I moan and grant him the access he requested. It doesn't take long for something simple to turn heated and needy.

Even though I've kissed other men, this is different. My cock is throbbing in my pants, and all I want is for my best friend to touch me there. Make me come undone.

The doorbell rings, and I curse under my breath. "Shit, I think that's the grocery order."

"I'll go get it. You keep cooking," he responds, heading to the door.

I take the moment of aloneness to adjust myself. I'm not sure if getting stopped when we did is a good thing or not. What I do know is it's going to be a long-ass day.

The baby monitor lights up as we finish putting the groceries away, Sammy's high-pitched cry coming through.

"I'll get him," Ford says, heading down the hall to rescue his son from the baby jail that is his crib.

After he walks away, I give the counters a final wipe-down.

By the time I'm done, footsteps sound down the hall, and the doorbell rings, which sends a jolt of anxiety through my veins. I'm not sure why, though. I like Mary. I shouldn't feel anxious about her arrival. Maybe it's because we're having such a great day so far, and she's the first person we're going to tell about our relationship in person. Hopefully, this goes well.

Chapter Twelve

FORD

DENVER OPENS THE DOOR with a giant smile on his face as I come down the hall, but it's a forced one. *Is he as anxious about this visit as I am?*

"Come on in," he greets Mary, stepping aside to let her into our house.

"What a lovely place this is," she says with a giant smile.

"Thanks, I bought it a few years ago," he tells her.

"That was a great buyer's market. Too bad it's so expensive now," she murmurs. "It will be harder for Ford to find a place without spending an arm and a leg."

"I'm not really in a hurry to move out," I supply.

"Well, you shouldn't wait too long. You and Sammy need a place of your own soon."

Sammy babbles, saving me from telling her about Denver and me just yet.

"Looks like someone's ready to see Grandma," I sing out.

"Oh, please let me hold him," Mary pleads, holding out her arms.

I carefully transfer over the bundle of joy, and Mary baby talks to him.

"Can I get you anything to drink?" I ask her.

She shakes her head. "I'm fine," she tells me while heading into the living room.

"Sammy loves singing and rocking. Why don't you have a seat and make yourself comfortable?" Denver suggests.

She smiles at him and carefully lowers herself into the recliner. Denver and I follow suit and sit beside each other on the couch.

"How has life with a newborn been treating you?" Mary asks us.

"Exhausting," I answer honestly.

Mary giggles. "I was a walking zombie with Samantha. She had terrible colic, and I never slept."

"I wonder if that's genetic," Denver voices. "Sammy was crazy difficult until we got him on his medication."

"Oh, what kind of medication?"

"Acid reflux. Apparently, it's common in babies, but I didn't think to ask if it was genetic," I supply.

"I didn't know babies could get that," Mary says, then makes a noise at Sammy.

"Neither did I, but the medication seems to be working. Every night seems to be better."

"That's wonderful. He sure seems happy."

"He is, and we're thankful for that."

"Being a parent is no joke," she states. "And the worries don't ever stop. Now I have to deal with the fact that my baby wants to move beyond forever away from here." Her lips turn downward, sadness written all over her face. I feel bad she's feeling this way, but I agreed to be on Samantha's side.

"Have you thought about moving with her?" I suggest, but Mary shakes her head.

"I'm too old to move," she mutters. "I was kind of hoping after Sammy was born, she'd change her mind. I mean, why would she move so far away from her child?"

Mary is busy staring at Sammy, and I shoot Denver a look, wondering how to respond. He shrugs in response, clearly as baffled as I am.

"Samantha doesn't see Sammy as her own," I say once my brain starts working again. "She only had him because it's what I wanted. You know she never wanted to be a mother."

She doesn't look convinced. "I know that's what she says, but I thought once Sammy was born, she'd change her mind. I mean, how can you hold this precious boy and not be wrapped around his fingers instantly? And the two of you have such a history together. After seeing you hold Sammy, I figured she'd see that letting you go was a mistake. Instead, she's still moving away, leaving you to raise this little man all on your own."

Shit, I didn't think Mary thought all of that. I assumed she understood what Samantha's and my agreement was.

"I'm not doing it on my own," I reply, giving Denver a smile and trying to steer things in a better direction.

"Friends are great, but don't you think Sammy deserves to have his mother in the picture?"

I take a deep breath, readying myself to tell her the truth.

"That isn't what Samantha wants. And Sammy isn't missing out on anything. He has all the love he needs."

"What about you?" Mary asks, cutting me off from getting to the other part I need to tell her. "Don't you want a partner? Someone who will be there through it all with you."

"Denver is my partner," I inform her, reaching for his hand. "It's new, but we're together."

Mary's eyes go wide, and she sucks in a breath. "I'm sorry..." she mutters. "I didn't know you were gay."

"We're both bi, actually," I correct her.

Mary nods but refuses to look either of us in the eye.

Casting a quick glance at Denver, I shoot him a look that says *What do we do now?*

He presses his lips together with wide eyes and shakes his head. *Great, he also doesn't know what to do.*

"I'm so sorry," Mary says, standing abruptly. "I completely forgot about an appointment I had. I should get going."

I swiftly move and take Sammy from her before she rushes out the door.

"Well, shit. That didn't go the way I thought it would," Denver mutters.

"I had no idea she felt that way," I respond. "I think I need to give Samantha a heads-up about this."

Denver nods, holding out his hands. "Give me Mr. Man. You go make the call," he suggests.

"Thanks." I let out a heavy breath, hand Sammy over, and head to my room.

Mary's response was so out of left field that I'm honestly left almost speechless. I mean, I wasn't sure how she'd take Denver and I being a couple, but I had no idea she wanted Samantha and I back together.

"Hello?" Samantha answers after a few rings, and my stomach turns to knots.

"Um... hey," I respond like an idiot, but the words I need to say don't want to come out.

"Is something wrong? Shouldn't my mom be there right now?" she questions.

"Um... yeah, she just left," I mutter.

"Oh no. What happened?"

"Well, she brought up you staying, like you thought she would, but it turns out to be more than that. She had it in her head that we were going to get back together."

"No..." Samantha says with a sigh. "Shit. Did you tell her about you and Denver?"

"Yeah, and she didn't take it too well. She made up a story about an appointment and hightailed it out of here."

"For fuck's sake," she mutters under her breath. "I'm so sorry she did that to you. I'll talk with her. I honestly thought she would accept your relationship. I didn't think she was homophobic."

"Maybe she just didn't want to let go of the idea of me and you together," I supply.

"It still doesn't make her lying and rushing away okay. I promise I'll talk with her, but also, no matter what happens, I'll still be in your life."

"Thanks, I appreciate it," I tell her, feeling a bit better but still hurt that Mary would leave like she did.

Once I end the call, I make my way to the living room, where Denver is playing with Sammy on the floor.

Although the meeting with Mary didn't go how I thought it would, it still doesn't stop me from thinking that life feels pretty damn perfect right now.

Watching my best friend—now boyfriend—play with my son like he's his own is something I never knew I needed in my life, and it's amazing.

Chapter Thirteen

DENVER

FORD IS TALKING GIBBERISH to Sammy, who's in his vibrating chair, when I put our plates on the table, ready for our lunch.

"How would you feel about an at-home date this evening?" I ask him as I sit beside him.

"What do you have in mind?" he asks with a smirk.

"Well, you planned our date last night. Let me take the reins on this one," I say.

Ford beams at me, nodding. "I can do that. You just tell me what I need to know, and I'll leave the rest up to you."

"After lunch, why don't you nap while Sammy does, and I'll get everything set up," I suggest, and my best friend's face lights up even more.

"I like this date already," he teases.

"Well, hopefully, I can really woo you later." I wink at him, and his cheeks turn a bright shade of red.

It's already so easy with Ford. The meeting with Mary threw us for a loop, but we aren't letting that hold us back. Some people aren't going to be okay with our relationship, but those people don't matter. I'm just hoping, for Sammy's sake, that Mary will come around.

Once we're done eating, Ford takes Sammy to get him ready for a nap, and I clean the kitchen.

"Are you sure you don't want help with anything?" he asks as I'm wiping down the table.

I shake my head. "Go nap. When you get up, I'll have everything ready for a perfect at-home date."

He smiles and walks over to me to give me a gentle kiss.

"You're already a perfect boyfriend," he whispers, making my heart do a funny flip.

I playfully shove him and wave my hand in the air. "Go. I have things I need to do."

He laughs and heads to his room. Once he's out of sight, I pull out my phone to come up with some ideas on what to do to make tonight extra special.

I snicker as I read through the lame date ideas people suggest before landing on the perfect one.

A game plan forms in my head, and an excited energy races through my body as I get to work. I've never felt this exhilarated for a date in my life.

A LOW WHISTLE PULLS my attention from my task of cutting up the last of the vegetables.

"Did you rearrange the entire house?" Ford teases.

"Well, you need kitchen chairs for the perfect blanket fort," I tell him with a shrug.

"I love it," he replies with the biggest smile I've ever seen.

"I was thinking we could go for a walk to the pond a few blocks away and have a picnic for dinner. After that, we'll come back for a movie in the blanket fort."

Ford's face lights up. "That sounds amazing."

My heart swells with pride that he likes my dorky plan.

The baby monitor lights up, and Ford heads to get Sammy ready while I pack the basket for our picnic.

It doesn't take me long to organize everything how I like it, so I take the basket outside and put it under the stroller while waiting for Ford and Sammy.

"Are you ready to be the third wheel on another date?" Ford asks Sammy as he exits the house with the cutest little boy ever.

"You're the best third wheel ever," I coo at him, taking him from his father's hold and placing him in the stroller while Ford locks up.

The weather is perfect as we walk to the pond, and I can't help but notice how happy I feel right now.

Who would have thought this would be my life?

"Thanks for planning this," Ford says, lifting one hand off the stroller and reaching for mine. Since this stretch is straight, it's easy to push with one hand, and it lets us be connected at the same time. As we transform from friends to more, the little shifts in our actions are sparking something in my heart.

"Well, you planned last night's date, and tomorrow you have to be back at work, so I wanted tonight to be special. Lord knows shit is about to get crazy around here soon."

Ford nods, but his face falls a little.

"I'm not looking forward to going back to work so soon. Hell, even the four weeks weren't going to be enough, but my partner needs me," he says.

I wrap my hand tighter around his, giving him a reassuring squeeze. "You're a great detective and an amazing father. We'll find a work-life balance soon," I reassure him.

After arriving at the pond, I set out a blanket and pull the basket out from under the stroller. When I'm done, Ford picks Sammy up and lays him down on the soft material.

"It's not a gourmet meal, but hopefully you like the food," I tell Ford as I set out the containers.

"Babe, we could be eating peanut butter and jelly sandwiches right now, and it would still be fucking perfect," he says.

God, this man always knows the perfect things to say. I'm sure my smile is fucking huge right now.

Sitting next to Ford and Sammy, we eat our food while laughing, talking, and simply spending time together. Who needs a fancy restaurant when you've got a perfect setting supplied by Mother Nature herself?

When we're done eating, we don't rush to clean up. Instead, we soak in the fresh air and the sounds of nature. We would spend more time outside if it weren't for Sammy getting uncomfortable.

"We should head back and get the little man a bath and a bottle," I suggest when Sammy's squawks grow louder.

Ford picks up his son, and as he gets him situated, I put the empty containers back in the basket.

"This was perfect. I can't wait for the second part of our date," Ford says as we make our way to the house.

"Why don't you get started on bath time? I'll put everything away," I offer as we walk up the front path.

Ford takes Sammy in while I get the basket out of the stroller and head to the kitchen.

After I finish putting away the last of the picnic items, I make a bottle for Sammy and head to the nursery, where Ford is swaddling the precious little baby.

"Come find me when you're done," I tell him, handing him the bottle and leaving them to have some bonding time. It also gives me time to make everything perfect.

With quick steps, I grab the iPad and baby monitor, place them in the fort, then head to the refrigerator to grab a tray of chocolate-covered strawberries I made earlier.

"Wow." Ford gasps when he enters the living room. Standing next to the fort, my cheeks heat a little with how happy and proud he looks. "You go all out when you plan a date," he notes.

"What can I say..." I pause for a second as butterflies erupt in my stomach. *Shit, I need to get myself under control.* "There is this guy I really like, and I wanted tonight to be extra special."

Ford chuckles, but the tone is low and throaty as he steps forward.

"So, are we *just* watching a movie tonight, or did you have something else planned?" he asks, slipping his hand around my waist.

"Want to make out like teenagers?" I tease.

Ford's eyes drop to my lips. "Could we do more than make out?" he asks.

My cock grows in my pants from his words. "What did you have in mind?" I ask, my voice wobbling from the lust rushing through my veins.

"How 'bout you get some supplies, and we'll see where the night takes us," he suggests,

I'm not sure he's even finished the sentence before I rush to my room to grab some lube and a packet of condoms. Ford's laughter follows me down the hall.

Once I'm back, he is already in the fort. Not wanting to keep my man waiting, I hastily set the supplies on the floor before opening the flap of the fort. I'm pleasantly surprised to find him in only his boxers, resting on the air mattress.

I wet my lips with my tongue as I take in this sexy man. I've ogled Ford many times before, but it was forbidden. Now, I get to watch to my heart's content. His perfect abs flex slightly, almost like they're begging to be licked, and that's exactly what I want to do.

"Oh, it's that kind of movie night, is it?" I ask, not moving farther in quite yet.

"Yep, and you're wearing far too much clothing. Strip and join me," he tells me.

I do as I'm told and climb in next to Ford, who promptly wraps his arms around me.

"What do you want to watch?" I ask, my heart racing in my chest.

"I'd rather not watch anything," he says, and my already hard cock twitches.

"What do you want to do, then?"

"I want to touch you," he whispers, leaning in for a kiss.

"Then touch me," I plead.

"How should I touch you?" he asks with mischievous eyes. "Like this?" His fingers trail up my arm, causing shivers of anticipation to run down my spine.

I shake my head, but I can't talk for some reason.

"What about this?" He moves to press his lips to my neck.

I whimper. "More."

Ford's tongue darts out to lick me as he moves up, pulling my earlobe between his teeth.

"Use your words, baby," he encourages me. My eyes roll into the back of my head. "What do you want?"

"I want to feel your skin on me," I blurt out.

He pushes me to lie down, following me so his body is on top of mine.

"Like this?" he asks as his chest presses against me.

I nod, wrapping my hand around his neck and pulling his lips to mine for a searing kiss. A moan escapes my lips as Ford pushes his hips forward, his hard cock rubbing against mine. The only barrier is the thin material of our boxers, and I want to get rid of them already.

Ford's tongue slides into my mouth, licking against mine as he grinds on me. I've always been pretty dominant in the bedroom, but fuck do I love the way Ford is taking charge right now. He's not allowing me any time to think.

It's exactly what I need.

After we make out for who knows how long, Ford rests his knees outside of mine and sits up so he's straddling me. He digs his fingers into my boxers, and I lift my hips, allowing him to get rid of them. Once they are pulled down, my cock springs free, making an audible thud against my abs. His strong, calloused hand wastes no time wrapping around my throbbing erection, and I throw my head back and cry out.

"You like that?" he whispers.

"Yes," I reply in a high-pitched tone. "So good."

"You're so fucking thick," he tells me, moving down my body.

I've had a dream like this before, but the reality is so much better.

Ford looks up at me as he sticks his tongue out, lapping at my crown. "Holy shit, you taste good," he murmurs before diving back in, this time slurping me into his warm, wet mouth.

"Shit!" I grab his head and try not to thrust into his mouth.

Ocean eyes stay locked on mine as my best friend gives me the perfect blow job. But it's when he gags that I almost stop him, not wanting to hurt him.

"It's fine," he assures me, obviously reading my expression. "You're just so goddamn big. Besides, I think I kind of like being gagged." I'm sure my eyes almost bug out of my head, and Ford chuckles. "Who knew sucking cock would be something I love so much?" he questions before going back to work.

A shiver breaks out low in my spine, the telltale sign that I'm close to blowing. I don't want this to end yet, so I roughly pull Ford up, smashing my lips to his as soon as he's within reach. The salty taste of my precum is on his tongue, and it makes me moan with need.

"My turn," I state as I roll us over.

I hastily get rid of his underwear and move to get a taste of him.

"Fuck, you look hot right now," he tells me, running his fingers through my short hair.

As a thank-you, I give his leaking cock a long, slow lick from root to tip, smirking as he grunts.

Once I'm at the crown, I swirl my tongue around, lapping at the precum there. The salty flavor explodes on my tongue, causing my own cock to leak again.

Shit, how come I didn't know how good this was?

It's not even the taste that's really doing it for me. It is the look of pure euphoria written all over Ford's face. I get to be the man who puts that look there. It's a heady feeling I could easily get addicted to.

After a few circles of the tip, I open my mouth and relax my jaw, taking him into my mouth. Ford's head falls back as he grips my hair a little tighter, causing a burn to my scalp that turns me on more.

I moan around him, and I'm positive he enjoys the vibration by the way he curses. Ford might not have the girth I do, but he's a hell of a lot longer than I am. I'm not sure I'll ever be able to take him all the way unless I figure out how to get rid of my gag reflex.

Lifting my right hand, I grip his base while sucking, using my fist to make up for the space I can't reach.

"Up," Ford demands, pulling out of my mouth.

I do as I'm told but can't stop the whimper before it escapes my lips.

"Why did you stop me?" I ask, feeling a little self-conscious.

"I didn't want to come yet," he responds with a sexy grin.

I chuckle, running my hand up and down his chest. "Can we try something?" I request, lying next to him.

"Anything," he responds.

The level of trust in his eyes right now is almost my undoing. Ford is too good for me, always has been, but like hell will I let him go without a fight.

I sit up, grabbing the lube I left on the floor at the entrance of the blanket fort. As I slick my cock, Ford's eyes glaze over with lust as he watches intently.

"Roll over and face me," I tell him, lying back down with him.

Even though I can tell he wants to fight for control, he does as I say.

Getting comfortable, I push my hips toward his, taking us both in my grasp.

"Fuck," Ford cries out as I jack us off together.

"Feels so good," I mumble.

Our cocks are pressed firmly together, and I'm not sure I've ever felt such a high from sex before. I don't know if it's because I've never done this with a man before or because I'm doing this with my best friend. I'm leaning toward the latter.

After I stroke us for a while, I buck into my fist, my cock sliding against his, which has us both moaning.

"Holy shit." Ford gasps, also thrusting.

It doesn't take long before a deep guttural roar rips past his lips, and he's coming all over us. The sight of his orgasm pulls me over the edge. I blow with a slew of curse words, coating us in a second layer of cum.

"Well, that was the hottest sex of my life," I murmur after a few heavy pants.

Ford chuckles and flops onto his back. "Want to shower with me? I don't think dried cum is going to be fun when it's matted into our hair."

I laugh along with him. "That sounds great. Do you want to come back to watch a movie or just go to bed?" I ask.

"Bed is probably the better plan. I do have to get up in the morning."

I nod and grab the baby monitor, leaving everything else behind. I'll deal with that tomorrow.

As we walk down the hall, I wait for another panic attack to take over, but it doesn't come. Instead, this comfortable calmness washes over me.

My best friend and I just had sex, and it was fucking perfect.

Chapter Fourteen

FORD

THE WATER IS STILL warming up when large hands slip around me, rubbing my chest.

"Why are you so fucking sexy?" Denver murmurs against me from behind. His stubble tickles me, sending jolts of need straight to my cock even though it's completely spent.

"I could ask you the same question," I respond, stepping into the shower and holding out a hand for my sexy boyfriend.

Wow, I still can't believe I get to call Denver my boyfriend. This is all so surreal.

Once we're inside and the door is closed behind us, I pull Denver toward me so we are both standing under the spray of water. My heart skips a beat, and a feeling of perfection seeps into my soul as he wraps his arms around me and rests his head on my chest.

"Has anything felt this right before?" I muse out loud.

"I was thinking the same thing," he replies before yawning.

"Come on, let's get washed quickly so I can hold you while we sleep," I suggest.

"Don't want to move," he murmurs.

I can't help but laugh. "The hot water isn't going to last long. Besides, I don't want you to drown."

He grumbles something unintelligible but moves so we can get clean. I pour some soap onto a loofah and wash Denver's chest, taking my time to clean the man who has always meant so much to me.

"No one's ever washed my body before," he whispers, watching me almost in awe.

"You deserve to be taken care of," I respond as I make my way down to scrub his balls.

"I'm too old to go for a second round so quickly," he tells me.

I chuckle. "Same. I'm just trying to get you clean," I reply before lightly smacking his hip. "Now turn around so I can do your back."

Something I've noticed tonight is Denver likes to be bossed around. At least in the bedroom, which is something I've always enjoyed doing. It's crazy how we click on so many levels. I knew there was a possibility we wouldn't mesh in bed, but so far, it turns out that, once again, we are perfect for each other.

Once Denver is clean, he takes the loofah from me, pours more soap on it, and takes his turn washing me. It's something so small, yet huge at the same time. It's intimacy on another level. My eyes never stray from him as he pays close attention to my entire body.

After our bodies are clean, we shampoo each other's hair. Neither of us is in a rush. My cock hardens as we occasionally brush up on one another, but as much as I'd love another round, I'm bone tired.

Newborns do that to a person.

I'm not sure how long we are in the shower, but eventually, the water turns cold, so we rinse off and rush out of the shower to warm fluffy towels waiting for us.

"Thank you for tonight," I whisper as we cuddle in Denver's bed.

As always, I check the baby monitor one more time before I allow myself to fully relax, thankful Sammy is still asleep.

"Thank you," he replies, then kisses my chest and snuggles in closer.

Having my best friend in my arms is how I want to end every single day from now on.

It doesn't take long for either of us to succumb to sleep.

I'M NOT SURE I'VE ever slept this soundly. Maybe that's why I startle awake when Sammy hasn't woken me up for some time.

"What's wrong?" Denver asks groggily as I rush to throw the blankets off us.

"Sammy hasn't woken in over four hours," I tell him, racing out of the room.

Denver is hot on my trail, knowing this isn't normal for our boy. He's up at *least* every two to three hours.

My heart beats so hard and fast I can feel it in my head, and my lungs struggle to take in a full breath as panic takes over my body.

Bursting into the nursery, I dash to the crib and place my hand in front of Sammy's face, fearing the worst.

When a burst of air from my tiny baby's nose hits my hand, I almost fall over from relief.

"He's alive," I whisper as tears pool in my eyes. "I know babies can sleep for longer stretches than a couple hours, but Sammy's never done it before," I murmur, even though Denver knows that already. "I was so fucking scared." I spin around, slamming into him, and hug him so tightly as I break down.

"It's okay," he whispers, rubbing my back and letting me have my freak-out. "It's normal to react like this. The doctor did say Sammy's sleep patterns could change with the medication we're giving him."

"She also said it could take up to a week to work," I reply.

"Well, thankfully, it didn't take that long. Poor little man needed the sleep as much as we did."

A small smile pulls at my lips.

"Why don't you change his diaper while I warm up a bottle?" Denver suggests. "Since we're awake, we might as well do the feed now. Maybe if we're lucky, we can get him back to sleep without a struggle and get another four-hour block of sleep."

The idea of sleeping that long again is heavenly.

"Thank you," I whisper, giving him a quick peck before letting him go.

I gently pick Sammy up and place him on the changing table. The glow of the soft night light illuminates the space enough so I don't have to turn on the main light and risk waking him too much.

I'm quiet as I clean my son, lost in my thoughts. He's only fourteen days old, but he's already my world. I might not be getting enough sleep, and the smell of poop makes me want to vomit, but I wouldn't change a thing because I get to have this perfect tiny human in my life.

Thankfully, Sammy stays still, so the diaper change doesn't take long. I'm finishing up the swaddle when Denver walks in like a knight in shining armor with a bottle of formula.

"You're the best," I tell him as I move to the rocking chair with Sammy in my arms.

"We're a team, remember?" he responds, and instead of fighting him like I have in the past, I only nod and smile.

"Why don't you head to bed? I'll join you when the little man is asleep," I promise, but he shakes his head.

"I'll wait for you." He leans against the wall, and I fall for him a little more. "Besides, you're really hot when you're in dad mode."

I chuckle, trying not to jostle Sammy too much, but he's so focused on eating that he doesn't seem to mind.

We don't talk much while our baby eats, but having Denver close makes the time pass a little faster.

"Come on, I'm ready to pass out again," I murmur after burping Sammy and putting him in his crib.

Right as the words leave my lips, a yawn slips out, and Denver laughs.

"Fingers crossed that Mr. Man sleeps for another good stretch," he whispers, almost as if saying the words too loud will jinx the situation.

Lacing my fingers through his, I pull him to his room and toward the bed.

Once we are comfortable again and Denver is back in my arms, I let my eyes shutter closed as I drift off.

If I had known holding this sexy bodyguard would get me to sleep so well, I would have suggested it sooner.

Chapter Fifteen

DENVER

FORD AND SAMMY ARE still asleep, so I carefully slip out of bed, making sure I don't disturb the man who held me all night. He still has a few hours before he has to leave for work and needs all the sleep he can get, especially after his middle-of-the-night panic attack.

Once I'm certain he's still sound asleep, I quietly leave to start breakfast, grabbing the baby monitor on the way out.

I'm not going to lie. I was also scared out of my mind when we raced to the nursery, but Ford needed me to be strong while he broke down. I've read many forums talking about what it's like the first time your baby sleeps for a longer period, but something about living it was a lot more terrifying.

I set the alarm on my phone to wake Ford, which is when Sammy will need his next feeding, then whip up some of my famous pancakes. I'm known for getting lost in thought, so I figured a reminder wouldn't hurt.

I'm pulling the last pancake from the frying pan when the chime on my phone goes off. I can't help but feel a sense of pride for timing that perfectly. I slip the dish into the oven beside the bacon to keep the food warm, hit start on the Baby Barista, and make my way to my room.

"Hey, babe, I hate to wake you, but breakfast is ready. I don't want you to be late for work," I say, leaning against the door frame.

"Okay, I'll be out in a minute," he murmurs in a sleep-laced voice. Next, I head to the nursery.

"Good morning, sleepy head," I sing, pulling Sammy out of his crib.

His little eyelids slowly blink open, but he doesn't look too happy to be woken from his peaceful rest.

"Let's get you changed, then you can have some yum-yums," I coo, placing him on the changing table.

Obviously, he doesn't respond, but the way he blinks at me gives me the impression he's thinking something along the lines of *Hurry up and get it over with already.*

As we're leaving the nursery, I'm greeted by a sleepy Ford. *Too bad he's already dressed.*

"Mornin'," he greets me before yawning and stretching his arms above his head.

The move allows his worn-out sleep shirt to rise, showing off his abs and delicious V from where his pajama pants hang low on his hips. Shamelessly, I let my eyes linger.

"Ready for breakfast?" I ask after I'm done ogling my man.

With a little pep in my step, I walk by him with the little bundle of joy in my arms, heading to the kitchen to grab the bottle.

"Want me to feed him?" Ford asks as I make my way to the living room to gently settle into the comfortable rocking chair.

I shake my head. "I was looking forward to our cuddle time," I tell him while pressing the nipple of the bottle to Sammy's lips.

"I'll grab a cup of coffee and keep you company," he states, heading to the kitchen.

Sammy guzzles his bottle like a pro as Ford sits on the sofa beside us. "How did you sleep last night?" he asks.

"Really good, but my body has a natural alarm clock, so I didn't really sleep in."

He nods, then brings the cup to his lips and takes a small sip. "So good," he murmurs into the mug.

I chuckle, trying not to jostle Sammy too much.

"How 'bout you? Did you sleep okay?" I check after staring at Sammy for a bit.

"The panic attack fucked me up, but having you in my arms is the best I've ever slept," he confesses.

My heart dances around in my chest at his words. I feel the same, but hearing it from him fills me with overwhelming joy.

"Well, I'm glad you got a few good hours of sleep," I reply. "Hopefully, your day is an easy one."

"I doubt it will be, but coffee gives me superpowers," he jokes. "How do you think Sammy's going to handle being at the office today?"

"I'm sure he's going to love it. Everyone there is looking forward to him hanging out."

Sammy finishes his bottle like a champ, and when he spits it out, I reposition him on my shoulder to pat his back. "Would you mind getting his medicine?" I ask Ford.

The smile my best friend gives me in response makes my mouth go dry. I've been really tuned into the smallest things about Ford since the accidental dick pic. I've gotten used to being turned on by the tiniest thing and having to fight a million emotions running through my head. Somehow that's only become stronger since his bi-awakening.

Thankfully, the emotions aren't as muddled anymore, and I'm no longer hating myself for being attracted to him.

"Is it wrong to admit how sexy you look rocking Sammy?" Ford inquires as he holds out the bottle of medicine.

I chuckle and shake my head. "Not if it's wrong to confess how just your smile turns me on," I reply, positioning Sammy back in my arms.

Ford laughs and gives his son the dose of medicine, which results in a not-so-happy face from Sammy.

"That doesn't taste good, does it?" I coo at Sammy before returning him to my shoulder.

The movement earns me a large belch, making us chuckle.

"I think he could win a burping contest with that one," Ford notes.

"Definitely. Takes after his father." My thoughts drift to a time in college when Ford actually did win a burping contest at a dive bar.

Keeping Sammy somewhat upright, I stand and walk to the kitchen.

"Ready for breakfast?" I call out to Ford, who's down the hall putting the medicine back in the nursery.

"Absolutely. My body is well caffeinated, and now I'm starving," he replies, walking into the kitchen. When he's close, he pulls Sammy from my arms and coos at him. "Who's the most handsome baby in the whole world?"

Damn, this man makes my heart melt.

"Why don't you put him on his play mat?" I suggest and move to grab two plates from the cupboard. "He could use some tummy time."

"Great idea. Mind dishing me up a plate?" he asks.

"Already on it," I respond with a smirk.

The sweet smell of pancakes and maple bacon assaults my senses as I open the oven, and I inhale deeply before pulling out the pans and dishing us up.

"Fuck, that looks amazing," Ford says, his words almost coming out as a moan as he takes a seat at the table.

"They taste even better," I tease, sitting beside him.

Ford takes a bite and *actually* moans. "Damn..." His eyes roll back a little as he savors the taste on his tongue.

"Didn't know my cooking was orgasmic," I joke, then take a bite of mine.

"Pretty fucking close, but I'll admit you know much better ways to make me come undone," Ford replies with a wink.

I try to fight the heat creeping up my cheeks, but I know the blush is taking over. I'm probably the shade of a tomato.

"I'm going to miss you guys," Ford whispers after we finish eating.

"We'll miss you too, but you've got an important case to work on, so don't worry about us, okay?"

He nods and leans in to kiss me. The kiss is simple, but it fills me with a warm feeling inside.

"I guess I better get changed," he murmurs before standing and trudging to his room.

My heart hurts for him as I know how hard today will be. Sammy is his world, and this is the first time the two are going to be apart like this. I wish it didn't have to be this way, but I will do everything I can to ensure Sammy has the best day ever.

I make a mental note to take lots of pictures.

It doesn't take Ford long to change, and my mouth waters at the sight of my man in a pair of slacks that showcase his ass in a delicious way and a form-fitting dress shirt that clings to his muscular chest.

Damn, that man cleans up well.

His gun is secured in his holster, and his keys are in hand as he saunters over to me for a goodbye kiss.

"Have a good day," he tells me before making his way over to Sammy to kiss him on the forehead. "Be good," he tells his son, then heads to the door.

"See you tonight," I call out as he leaves the house with a wave.

It's the first day of our new routine, and I hope it goes well.

Chapter Sixteen

FORD

My steps are heavy as I walk into the station and head for the office I share with my partner. As much as I love my job and know how important it is, I don't want to be here.

I want to be home with my son, experiencing all his firsts.

But at least he's in good hands.

"Welcome back," Melody sings out.

I offer a tight smile in return, causing the one that was brightly shining on her face to fall.

"What's wrong?" she asks with furrowed brows.

"I just miss Sammy already."

A look of understanding appears on her face. "It's not easy coming back to work after having a baby. I remember I was a mess the first month back after Keely was born. As I said on the phone, I hate that I had to call you back earlier than we agreed, but this case has gotten insane."

I nod, already knowing a bit about what's going on from our phone calls. "It's okay. I know you didn't pull me away from my son on purpose. How 'bout you give me a full rundown on what we're dealing with?"

"Heather Anderson's body was discovered a few days after you went on paternity leave," she starts like she told me on the phone the other day.

"What did the coroner find?" I ask, hating that she died.

She was only thirteen.

A spark of rage lights up Melody's eyes as she grinds her back molars, the sound audible.

"Whoever took her was a sick fuck," she grumbles. "Not only was she raped, but she was tortured as well."

My blood boils. "Do we have any leads as to who it was?"

She shakes her head and grabs a piece of paper off her desk. "No, but this is why I needed you back," she says, handing me a photograph of the dead girl.

I clench my free fist as I take in all of the marks on the innocent child's body, but what is circled really draws my attention.

In the middle of her chest is the number two engraved into her chest.

"What the fuck is that supposed to mean?" I question, my voice louder than I intended it to be.

"I think it means she's the second victim," Melody replies, rifling through more papers. "Two months before Heather disappeared, there was another girl who went missing. Stefanie Tudor. Her body was discovered a month later. She was also raped and tortured, and a number one was engraved on her chest." She hands me another picture.

"For fuck's sake," I grit out, my teeth grinding so hard my jaw hurts. "We're dealing with a fucking serial killer here?"

Melody frowns. "I think so. Again, that's why I needed you back. We have to figure out how the girls are connected so we can stop this from happening again and catch the perp."

I drop the papers on Melody's desk and run my hands over my face. "What have you found out so far?" I inquire, ready to get down to business.

"Not a whole lot. I've just started going through Stefanie's case, but nothing is jumping out at me."

"Can you give me the list of those who were already questioned?" She shuffles things around on her desk before handing over the papers. "Keep digging through the case. I'll get to work reinterviewing these people," I instruct.

So much for hoping today was going to be an easy day.

MY HEAD IS KILLING me when I walk through the door later, but the scent of garlic, dill, and other spices fills my nose and brings a small smile to my lips.

"What smells so good?" I ask Denver as he's pulling something out of the oven.

"Chicken lasagna," he replies, looking over his shoulder with bright eyes and a giant grin. "How was work?"

I sigh. "Long."

I head to my room to secure my gun before heading to the living room and making my way over to Sammy, who is having some tummy time. "How was your day, Mr. Man?" I babble at my son, whose answer is to spit at me. "Sounds like a good one," I say as if he had actually responded. "Was he okay at the office?"

"He was excellent, although I didn't really see him all that much. He was stolen by almost every employee at Hunter Security at some point throughout the day," he informs me, which warms my heart.

"I'm so glad he had a bunch of people to love on him today."

"He absolutely did," Denver assures me. "Now come on, let's eat. You look like you're about to pass out."

After I pick up Sammy, I follow my man to the kitchen, gently place my son in his vibrating chair, and sit at the table. My stomach growls so loud it makes Denver laugh.

"Did you eat at all today?" he teases, placing our plates on the table and sitting beside me.

I have to think about the question for a minute. "I got a sandwich at some point and a few protein bars," I tell him. "It was a crazy day, though, and I doubt my days will slow down anytime soon."

"Do you want to talk about it, or would you prefer to just leave it at work?" he asks, making my heart do a funny flip.

It's a simple question, but it is reassuring that he isn't pressuring me to spill about what's going on. "I'd like to leave it for tonight," I reply.

Denver reaches over to squeeze my knee. "Then that's what we'll do. How 'bout I tell you about Sammy's adventures?"

I smile. "That would be great."

He goes on to tell me about Sammy throwing up all over Knox when he was burping him and him having a massive shit that made Sophie gag. The stories continue while we eat our supper, and I couldn't ask for a better end to my day. Spending it with the man who's always been my ride-or-die and is now becoming more, plus the most perfect baby, is all I could wish for.

Denver grabs our plates after we've both finished, and I take Sammy to his room to get him out of his dirty clothes before carrying him to the bathtub.

Sammy splashes in the tiny tub while I clean him and sing him a few songs.

"I'm surprised he doesn't cry when you sing," Denver jokes, leaning against the door as I'm drying Sammy off.

"I'm not that bad," I retort and stick my tongue out at him.

"Want me to get his bottle ready?" he asks.

I beam at him. "That would be wonderful."

I stand with my son wrapped in a blanket and turn to my boyfriend for a gentle kiss before we both head in opposite directions.

By the time I'm finished dressing Sammy and starting the swaddle, Denver is back with a perfect bottle and an even better smile.

"I'm so lucky to have you in my life," I confess while wrapping my sleepy little boy.

"I'm the lucky one," he replies, striding over to us to press a gentle kiss on Sammy's head.

"Where's mine?" I ask with a cheeky grin.

Denver shakes his head at my teasing but appeases me with a kiss of my own.

"Would you like to sleep in my room tonight, or do you want some space?" he asks as I sit in the rocking chair and adjust my bundled-up baby in my arms.

"I don't need space," I assure him as I reach for the bottle.

"Perfect. I'll see you there," he states, then leaves me to have some alone time with my son.

Being away from him all day was torture, especially after having to talk to the parents of the other murdered girl. I felt sympathy for the parents before, but now, having my own son, my perspective has changed.

I don't know how I'd survive if anything happened to Sammy. He's my life. It makes me that much more determined to solve these cases and put the asshole responsible for it all behind bars. The families of these girls deserve answers, and I'm determined to get them.

I'm not sure how long passes before Sammy spits out the bottle, and I lift him to my shoulder for a good burping. Fingers crossed, he sleeps as well as he did last night. After a long day like I had, I'm going to need all the sleep I can get.

Sammy lets out a loud belch, and I chuckle, laying him down in his crib before quietly leaving the nursery and shutting the door behind me. Then I stop in my room to quickly grab a change of clothes before heading to Denver's.

The sound of running water alerts me that he's in the shower, which gets my blood rushing south.

Hopefully, he wants company.

With long strides, I make my way through the open bathroom door, stripping out of my clothes before pulling the shower curtain back. "Mind if I join you?" I ask with a flirty tone and am beyond thrilled when he shoots me a sexy smile.

"I was wishing you would," he responds, reaching out his hand for mine.

I gladly take it, allowing him to pull me into the shower with him. The hot water immediately soothes my sore muscles, and I let out a contented sigh.

"You're sexy when you're wet," Denver informs me with a wicked grin before placing his other hand behind my head and giving me a gentle tug.

When his lips touch mine, I release a needy moan and melt into him. My body relaxes as if this is what I needed all day.

Letting go of his hand, I wrap mine around his waist, pulling him even tighter to me, not wanting any space between us. As soon as he's pressed against me, I deepen the kiss, licking the seam of his lips, demanding entrance. I rejoice on the inside when he gives it to me so willingly.

A low growl of protest forms in my throat as Denver moves his hips back briefly, but a moan quickly replaces it as his large, calloused hand wraps around my cock.

"I missed you today," I tell him, breaking for air.

"It's crazy, but I did too. How have we already become needy partners in the honeymoon stage of a relationship? You'd think our long friendship would make things different."

I'm about to respond when he tightens his grip on my cock, and a desperate mewl leaves my lips. My toes curl as a jolt of lust shoots down my spine, straight to my balls.

"I'm not going to last long," I confess, but I almost want to cry when he releases me. "I didn't mean stop," I complain.

Denver chuckles and pushes his hips forward, this time gripping us both together in his fist. "I wanted in on the action too," he replies.

My eyes roll into the back of my head as he thrusts into his grip, his rock-hard cock rubbing against mine.

"Feels so good," I moan as he jacks us off together.

"You're so fucking hot when you're about to come," he tells me before smashing his lips to mine again.

The kiss is hot and needy, mixed with bites and a few clashes of teeth as we both try to take what we need.

Denver's hand never slows. We both buck into his grip as our releases draw near. I'm not sure who comes first, but warm cum covers our abs, and my head spins a little with how intense the orgasm was.

"Is it always going to be this amazing?" I ask.

"I fucking hope so," Denver responds as he moves to grab his loofah.

With gentle hands, he washes my body. I love that he knows exactly what I need right now and how to make me feel better.

We've only been dating for a couple of days, but right now, it's obvious that I'm already falling head over heels for my best friend.

Chapter Seventeen

DENVER

Margret reaches her hands out to me while wiggling her fingers the second I step into the office on Monday morning.

"Do you want a hug?" I tease, resulting in an eye roll from my colleague.

"If you don't give me that baby in three seconds, I'm quitting," she threatens.

I laugh as I set the carrier down and unclip Sammy. Once he's free from the car seat, I hand him over to Margret.

"See? I'm a valuable employee here. No one wants me to quit," she coos at the baby.

I shake my head with a giant smile on my lips. "I'm going to check my emails. As soon as you get sick of Sammy, let me know, and I'll rescue you."

She cackles and shoos me off.

Not wanting to piss the woman off, I turn on my heels and head for my office. There is a strong chance I won't hear a peep from her until I take a break and hunt her down.

With my office just off the reception area, I hear Margret singing to Sammy as I turn my computer on, making my smile grow even wider. I'm beyond lucky I can bring the little man to the office, and I know it puts Ford's mind at ease.

It's been two weeks since he's been back at work, and to say it's been a shit show would be an understatement. The case he's working on is driving him up a wall. The only thing I can do is relieve a bit of his stress at night, which is no trouble for me. I've been enjoying finding new ways to make him let go and forget how fucked-up the world we live in is, even if only for a few minutes.

However, I hate how much this case is getting to him. I don't know much about it since Ford doesn't like bringing work home with him, but I know enough. A serial killer is targeting young girls, and everywhere Ford and his partner turn, they keep hitting dead ends.

I've worked stalker cases where we couldn't figure out who the hell was behind it, which was stressful enough. This is a whole other level. I feel so fucking bad for him.

Shaking my head, I try to focus on the tasks I need to get done. There isn't anything I can do for Ford right now, so I just have to let it go and pray they can solve the case quickly.

Opening my emails, I let all other thoughts go and hyperfocus on the task at hand.

I'm not sure how much time has passed when my phone rings. I grab it off the desk and mutter under my breath as my mom's picture and name light up on the screen.

Shit, is it that time already?

"Hey, Mom," I answer with a cheery tone, praying she'll forgive me for forgetting to pick her up at the airport.

"I'm billing you for the rideshare I'm already in," she tells me with a bratty tone.

I let out a sigh of relief. "I'm sorry, I forgot to set an alarm. Life has been so crazy, and then I got lost in my work this morning."

"It's fine, sweetheart," she assures me. "I just wanted to let you know I'll be at your office in half an hour."

"I'll finish what I'm working on and take off the rest of the after-noon," I tell her, but she clicks her tongue at me.

"Don't do that. Finish your day. I'll hang out with Margret, or maybe Sophy can show me how to work Photoshop again. There are a few things I'm stuck on."

I chuckle and run a hand over my face. My mom and Sophy togeth-er are plain old trouble. The last time they hung out, Sophy taught my mom how to put my head on animal bodies, and they made a million memes. It was funny at first, but it got old quickly.

"I'll see you in a bit," I tell her before sharing quick I love yous and ending the call.

Pushing my chair back, I head to the front, where Margret is talking on the phone, and Sammy is sleeping in the playpen behind her desk.

"He's a perfect baby," she states once she hangs up.

"He really is," I agree. "So, I'm a horrible son and forgot to pick my mom up from the airport, but she's in a rideshare on her way here now."

Margert laughs loudly. The noise must startle Sammy because he moves but thankfully doesn't wake up. "Shit, I have to remember not to be so loud," she murmurs. "Are you taking the afternoon off, then?"

"No, Mom wants to hang out with you and Sophy, but I do plan on heading home a little early."

She beams at me, but it has an eerie feel to it. *What is that woman thinking?*

"Oh, that sounds like a fantastic day. Now I won't have to resched-ule the client I just got off the phone with."

"Someone new?" I inquire.

She nods, her smile now disappearing. "A young influencer who has a stalker. Poor thing is only twenty, but she's blown up on social media and now has someone who won't leave her alone."

"Send me her information. I'll run a background check before she gets here."

"Absolutely. She'll be here at two, so you'll have time to visit with your mom beforehand."

"I'm sure she'll be all about Sammy and forget I even exist," I joke, earning me a heartfelt chuckle from Margret. "Can you let me know when she gets here?"

Once she nods in acknowledgment, I make my way to my office, and within a few minutes, the information for our new client arrives in my inbox.

Emelia Margot.

Twenty years old

Birthday: June 30th

Born in a small town in Tennessee

Moved here when she was sixteen

Net Worth: twenty million dollars

My eyes almost bug out at the last part. I'm aware influencers these days can make a lot of money, but that is more than a lot.

After putting her information into our background tracking software, I wait for it to pull up everything known about Emelia Margot. It doesn't take long for news reports to start popping up, but my heart sinks at the information I find.

Emelia's mother was murdered by her father when she was only ten. After Mr. Margot stabbed Mrs. Margot multiple times, he took his own life with a bullet to the head. Emelia was found by a neighbor sometime after, wandering down the street. According to reports, the household was never stable, and multiple reports to children's services had occurred before the fatal incident.

After that, there isn't much information on Emelia until she started blowing up on social media at eighteen. It looks as if she was almost an overnight success. Her account is a mixture of fashion, travel, makeup, and women's rights.

I scroll through her account, noticing some comments that throw up red flags for me. They all have a similar creepy vibe but are never by the same person. If I had to guess, it's the same person with multiple burner accounts. The accounts have no information, pictures, or anything. When I find an email, again, I hit a dead end for information.

Once I feel like I have enough information on Emelia for the time being, I send the file to the office cloud and call Knox.

"Hey, man, what's up?" he answers after a few rings.

"Can you come into the office at two?" I ask. "We've got a new client coming in. You would be a good fit for her."

"I should be able to swing that. What kind of client?"

"Twenty-year-old influencer with a stalker. I think she'll be a full-time job."

He lets out a low whistle. "Damn. Sounds intense, but you know I'm always up for a challenge."

"So, I'll see you at two?" I check.

"Absolutely," he says and ends the call.

After placing my phone on the desk, I pull up our scheduling software and block Knox out for the foreseeable future. Thankfully, I didn't have him scheduled for any events this week, so I only have to move a few things around later in the month. Our newest bodyguard, Hendrix, will be able to fill in for those.

By the time I've updated the schedule, I hear laughter and chatter coming from the front. A warm voice that instantly puts me at ease filters down to my office.

I rush out to greet my mom.

"There's my baby boy," Mom coos at me as if *I'm* the baby in the room.

"Not so much a baby anymore," I grumble, but there is a smirk on my lips as I pull her into my arms for a big hug.

"You'll always be my baby," she whispers into my ear before kissing my cheek. "Now show me the new baby."

A tiny squawk sounds from behind Margret's desk, and I make my way to Sammy, lifting him gently.

"Meet Sammy," I tell Mom, who reaches out for him, but I shake my head. "Let me change him first."

She follows me to my office, where I have a changing station set up in the corner.

"He is so cute," Mom admires as I lay Sammy down. "He looks so much like Ford."

"I see a good mixture of Ford and Samantha, but he has Ford's ocean-blue eyes," I say as I change a squirmy Sammy.

"He's got his scowl too," Mom points out, and I laugh. She isn't wrong. "How is Ford doing, by the way?"

"He's working an intense case right now and hates being away from Sammy, but other than that, good. He's excited to see you after work tonight."

She smiles as I pick up Sammy and finally hand him to her.

"You are the most perfect baby ever. I am going to spoil you forever and ever," she babbles at Sammy. Watching her with him warms my heart.

"Did you eat before you got here?" I question. She shakes her head, so I go to my desk and grab my phone. "How 'bout I order us something? I forgot to pack my lunch today as I accidentally slept in."

"Sammy still keeping you up at night?" she inquires. "I thought his acid reflux medication was working."

Heat rushes to my cheeks, and I grab the back of my neck. Yeah, it wasn't Sammy who kept me up last night, but I can't exactly tell Mom that. I'm still not one hundred percent positive about how we're going to tell her that Ford and I are dating.

We'll cross that bridge tonight when I have the support of my partner.

"Sammy sleeps like the dead now. I just had a hard time falling asleep," I fib.

Mom doesn't seem to notice I'm a bit out of sorts, her attention solely on Sammy.

"How 'bout I make you a special tea tonight? You'll fall asleep as soon as your head hits the pillow," she assures me.

"I'm sure I'll be fine. What do you want for lunch?" I ask, changing the topic.

After we pick what we are going to eat, Mom heads off with Sammy safely in her hold to find Sophy, and I finish a few projects I had on the go while waiting for the food.

EMELIA SHOWS UP AT exactly two, and I'm at the front, ready to greet her.

"It's nice to meet you," I say, reaching out to shake her hand.

She takes it with a forced smile. "I wish we didn't have to meet like this."

Even though she's wearing makeup, which is probably covering up the dark circles under her eyes, it's obvious how tired she is. It's hard not to feel bad for her.

"I understand. Why don't you join me in our boardroom? Knox is waiting there for us." She nods and follows me to the room, where

I shut the door behind us. "Emelia, this is Knox," I introduce him. "He'll be your bodyguard if you hire us. We have a few questions we need to ask you before we get started."

She chews on her lower lip, and her eyes dart around the room. It's obvious she's anxious to be here.

"I'll tell you whatever you want to know as long as you can promise me you'll keep me safe," she mutters and reaches into her purse. "He left this on my pillow this morning." She pulls out a single rose. When she looks back at me, there are tears in her eyes. "He got into my *house.* Who knows what will happen next?"

Knox's teeth audibly grind, and his face turns red, his disgust clear.

"We'll keep you safe *and* catch this sicko," he vows to her.

"At least you don't think I'm crazy," she whispers.

"Why don't you start from the beginning? Tell us the whole story," I instruct. "Don't leave out any details. The more we know, the better."

She closes her eyes and takes a deep breath. After she lets it out, she stares at us both, pure determination written all over her face as she gives us the complete rundown.

It turns out this stalker has been around for almost a year but recently has stepped things up.

"Did you keep all the gifts?" Knox asks after Emelia finishes.

"A friend of mine told me to throw them out, but I figured they might be helpful for the police. Turns out, the police think I'm crazy and refuse to do anything about this," she responds, then lets out a frustrated sigh.

"They are stuck with a lot of red tape they have to walk through, but we aren't," I inform her.

"I understand that, but what more *proof* do I need?" she asks, exasperated. "I don't want to die."

The tears are back, and she's shaking now.

"We won't let you die. I promise," Knox assures her.

"I'm gonna hold you to that," she says, holding intense eye contact with him.

"Since your house isn't secure, I'm going to insist you stay at a hotel until we can fix that," I start. "Due to the severity of your situation, we recommend full-time security. Knox will be with you twenty-four seven, except for his days off, then one of our other bodyguards will be with you. If, for whatever reason, Knox or any of our other bodyguards aren't a good fit for you, please let me know. We will address your concerns and make changes with no hard feelings."

This seems to make Emelia relax a little, and she nods.

"Our tech team will also need access to all of your social media accounts so we can try to figure out who your stalker is and put an end to this."

"I appreciate this all more than you could ever know," she tells me.

"Do you have a personal assistant or others who are close to you?" Knox asks.

"I used to have a personal assistant, but she was a bitch and leaked personal photos of me. I had to let her go."

"Can we have her information, please?" I request. "I'd like to look into her to see if she could have any connections with the stalker."

"I considered that also, but I can't connect them in any way. I'll give you her details, though. Maybe your tech team will be able to come up with something I was missing."

"We've got the best working here at Hunter Security. You'll be in good hands," I assure her.

"Consider yourselves hired," she says, pushing her chair back.

"Did you drive here?" Knox asks.

"I might be rich, but I'm kind of guarded. I like to keep my circle small. That means no driver for me."

"You have one now," Knox replies with a smirk. "Why don't you call a hotel and get a room? I'll grab my bag from my car, and then we can head to your place so you can pack."

"I'll arrange for our team to set up a security system at your house as soon as possible so you aren't out for too many days," I add.

"I'm not going to lie and say this is easy for me, but if it's what I have to do, so be it," she states.

We go over a couple more details, then Emelia books a hotel room for her and Knox. Shortly after that, they leave, and I go to the front to find my mom.

"Ready to go home?" I ask her as I walk up to the reception desk.

She smiles and shrugs. "I'm ready whenever you are."

I chuckle, reaching to take Sammy from her. "Well, I'm ready," I assure her as I put the tiny baby in his car seat.

I still can't believe he's a month old already. Time is flying by.

Chapter Eighteen

FORD

As I OPEN THE door, the sound of laughter floats out of the house. Two smiling faces greet me from the living room. My heart flutters, but there is also a mixture of anxiousness there.

It's been amazing to come home to Denver every night and being met with a kiss or a warm hug. I'm actually craving his touch right now, but I can't hold him quite yet, which sucks.

"Daddy's home," Mama Rachel tells Sammy as she stands and rushes over to me.

When I lived with them as a kid, she constantly refused to go by Mrs. London, and it didn't feel right to just call her Rachel, so we landed on Mama Rachel, a habit I don't think I'll ever break, even now that I'm an adult.

When she reaches me, she pauses, places her hands on my shoulders, and gives me a good look over. "You need more sleep," she states before pulling me in for a hug.

"It's good to see you too," I mutter, resulting in a giggle from her.

"Oh, you know I've missed my boys, but the mother in me is never gonna overlook those bags under your eyes."

I shrug and kiss her on the cheek. "I'd expect no less from you. If you'll excuse me, I'm going to secure my gun and change," I tell her.

"Perfect, dinner will be ready when you come out," she says, and I make my way to the bedroom.

"How was your day?" Denver asks, entering the room as I pull on a pair of gray sweats.

"More dead ends," I respond with a sigh.

He closes the distance between us and pulls me into his arms. "I'm sorry you're going through this, but I'm here if you ever need to vent."

I hold him for a moment, relishing in the comfort he gives me.

"Have you figured out how we are going to tell your mom we are together?" I ask after we separate.

"I think we should rip the Band-Aid off," he suggests.

A tingle runs through my arms, and my stomach churns. *What if she reacts like Mary did?*

"Take a deep breath," Denver urges. It's then I realize I'm barely breathing, so I do as I'm told. "She isn't Mary." It's as if he's reading my mind. "Mom might be shocked, but she isn't going to have a bad reaction."

I nod and take another deep breath, filling my lungs to capacity before slowly letting it out. "Okay, let's do this."

Denver's smile eases some of my nerves. He gives me one more hug before leaving me to finish getting dressed.

"Something smells good in here," I call out as I walk into the kitchen.

"Denver helped me make meatloaf," Mama Rachel tells me with a warm grin.

"Well, I can't wait to eat it," I tell her as my stomach rumbles loudly.

Mama Rachel laughs, tilting her head toward the table. "Sit, it's almost done."

I pull up a seat next to Sammy in his vibrating chair.

"Did you have a good day, Mr. Man?" I coo at him.

His response is to spit at me, but I take it as *It was good*.

Denver sets a plate in front of me and takes the empty chair beside me while his mom sits across from us.

"Ford and I wanted to tell you something," Denver says after we take a few bites.

"What's that?" she asks with her signature inviting grin.

It's the look that used to get me to spill my guts as a kid. She has this way of making everyone feel safe. It's something I've always loved about her. Even though there are still some nerves bouncing around inside me, I'm somewhat calmer.

"We're dating," I tell her.

Denver grabs my hand with a smile, and Mama Rachel's eyes go wide before her face lights up.

"This isn't a joke, is it?" she questions, studying both our faces.

"No, Mom, I'd never joke about this. It's new and something neither of us were expecting, but we're happy," Denver assures her.

"Then I'm happy for you. Honestly, it makes a lot of sense. You two have always been inseparable. Also, it explains why Ford's room looks as if no one has been in there in weeks."

It didn't take us long to decide to move my stuff into Denver's room since we spent every night together. We couldn't see the point of having separate spaces anymore.

"You were snooping?" Denver asks.

His mom shrugs. "I'm surprised you're shocked at that. It's like you don't even know me," she teases.

Finally, the weight that was resting on my shoulders releases, my stomach unknots, and I feel like I can breathe again.

"Samantha also wasn't surprised when we told her," I mention.

"Have you told Mary yet?" she asks.

I look down at my table as pain radiates through my chest. "She didn't take it so well," I mutter.

Mama Rachel gasps. "I didn't take her for a homophobe."

"Neither did we," Ford replies.

His brows are pulled together, and his lips are turned downward. Anger radiates off him, so I squeeze his hand.

"I'm still not sure that it's straight-up homophobia," I voice.

They both look at me like I've grown a second head.

"Think about it. She had this idea in her head that Samantha and I would get back together and be this happy little family, but now that Denver and I are together, that dream is shattered. I'm not saying her reaction was right, but maybe she's just processing. I'd rather her walk away and take time to deal with her feelings than say something she can't take back."

Mama Rachel nods. "I see where you're coming from. Hopefully, she comes around."

Denver doesn't look as convinced, but I have this feeling that whatever is going on with Mary will sort itself out. She isn't a bad person, simply confused. If she doesn't come around, that's on her, and we'll just have to live with it. We can't force everyone to accept this.

Dinner is filled with easy conversation sharing what's new, and it makes me happier than I've ever been.

Once we are finished eating, I take Sammy to his room to change and get ready for bed while Denver and Mama Rachel clean up.

"Who's ready for their bottle?" Denver asks when I finish swaddling my son.

Sammy's lips smack together, and I chuckle.

"It's nice having your mom here," I tell him as I take the bottle and settle into the rocking chair.

Leaning against the wall, Denver nods. "It really is, and she's very happy for us..." He pauses and smiles. "I knew she would be accepting, but I'll admit, I was the tiniest bit nervous that it might take her a minute."

"I think that's normal, especially with how Mary reacted," I supply.

"Does it make you wonder how other people in our lives are going to react?" he asks.

I tilt my head. "A little, but we surround ourselves with open-minded people. If someone has a problem with us being together, I don't want them in our lives anyway."

"I love how well you're taking this," he whispers.

Sammy spits out his bottle then, and I put him on my shoulder to burp him.

"What we have feels more *right* than anything else has in my entire life. I refuse to ignore that feeling."

He beams at me and steps toward us. "I'll meet you in our room," he whispers before kissing me gently.

Shortly after Denver leaves, Sammy burps, and I kiss his head before laying him in his crib.

"Is your mom already in bed?" I ask when I enter our room.

"Yeah, she was tired. She also has our entire day planned tomorrow, so she wanted to be well-rested for a busy day."

"I wish I could join you," I mutter, pulling my shirt off.

"I know, but your job is important. We'll make up for the missed moments once you solve this case," he assures me.

Moving forward, I close the space between us and pull him into my arms.

"I don't know what I'd do without you," I whisper into his hair.

"Good thing you never have to find out."

"Come have a shower with me," I request, taking a step back.

"Are you sure? Because we've yet to have a shower without getting frisky," he reminds me with a mischievous smirk.

"I can be quiet," I respond, grabbing his hand and tugging him to the bathroom.

He chuckles and lets me lead him into the en suite.

"How is it that it's only been approximately twelve hours since I've had you, yet it also feels like an eternity?" he asks, stripping out of his clothes as I do the same.

"I feel the same way. I need you so bad, baby." My voice is husky, and my cock grows at the sight of the sexy man in front of me.

Denver moves to turn on the water, setting it to the right temperature before stepping in and holding out his hand for me. As soon as I take it, I'm pulled into a passionate kiss. His tongue licks at the seam of my lips, so I eagerly let him in.

Fuck, I love the taste of him and the way he melts into me when we kiss.

The water runs over us as we make out and grind into each other.

"Turn around," I command. The man who has stolen my heart does as he's told. "Hands on the tile, baby."

Once he's in position, I kneel behind him, pressing a kiss to his bubble butt before pulling his cheeks apart and running my tongue over his pucker. Both of us moan at the same time, and my cock leaks.

One of the many things I've discovered these past few weeks of being together is that I love to eat Denver's ass.

"You like that?" I ask before diving back in, pushing my tongue through the tight muscles of his hole.

"Mm-hmm" is his response, making me giddy with pride.

I love that I get to turn a normally well-spoken man into a mumbling mess. It's a heady feeling.

Wanting to make this feel even better for him, I suck on my fingers before urging one into his tight channel.

"Yes... fuck... more..." Denver pleads as I stretch him, slowly pressing in a second finger.

"Stay quiet, baby," I whisper before lapping at his hole and shoving my tongue in with the digits.

Once he's decently stretched, I reach for the bottle of lube we've kept in the shower since we started regularly messing around in here and grab the dildo I bought last week from the shelf we've been keeping it on.

The thought of his mom possibly being in here pops into my head, causing a shudder to run down my spine. "I hope your mom didn't snoop too well."

"Fuck... don't bring my mom up when you're fucking me," he grumbles.

I chuckle as I pour lube on the dildo and press it to his beautiful pucker. I've been dying to get my cock inside him, but both of us want to take our time when we take that next step, and time has not been on our side recently.

"You're so fucking hot," I tell him as I work the dildo inside him. His head falls forward, resting on the tile as hot pants escape his lips. "Turn for me. I want to suck your cock," I say.

Like usual, he willingly obeys the order.

Moving my hand so it's between his legs, I continue to fuck him with the dildo as I stick my tongue out to lick at the tip of his dick.

Denver moans as I circle his crown. His hands find purchase in my hair, giving a small tug that has my cock twitching.

"You are so good at that," my best friend tells me.

I smile around him, taking him deeper into my mouth.

If someone had told me a month ago that sucking Denver's cock could become an addiction, I would have told them they were crazy, but it is true. Having his giant dick inside my mouth is something I crave daily.

My lips stretch, and my jaw aches, but when the man in front of me loses control, thrusting his hips forward and pushing more of himself into my mouth, I'm filled with a feeling of euphoria.

I bob up and down, swallowing him deep, as I fuck him with the dildo. My ragingly hard dick leaks like a fucking sieve between my legs as I suction around his length, pulling magnificent moans from him.

I've always enjoyed giving pleasure to my partners, but I never knew I could almost get off from it before. That's what Denver does to me. Simply making him come undone is damn near enough to make me blow my load.

"Don't stop," Denver begs as I swallow him.

I gag, taking in as much of him as I can, refusing to pull away because I know it will drive him wild to feel my throat spasm around his cock head. Having him blocking my airway makes me slightly lightheaded, but it also heightens my need to come, edging me to the brink of orgasm.

With how Denver is panting and moaning, I know he's just as close, so I adjust the angle of the toy, hitting his prostate. He bucks forward at the added sensation and instinctively grabs my head, moving us together. I pick up the speed of my hand, fucking him faster with the dildo and sucking as hard as I can. I want his load in my mouth *now*.

"Shit... fuck... I'm... gonna..." he mutters, trailing off as his orgasm takes over his body, and his cum shoots down my throat and fills my mouth.

Quickly using my free hand to grab my shaft, I jerk off while greedily swallowing every drop. I'm almost embarrassed that it only takes a couple of tugs before I unload onto the shower floor, but I'm really not.

"You are so amazing," Denver whispers after I've pulled the dildo out of his ass, and he helps me to my feet.

I kiss him passionately and hold him until the water temperature drops, and we both shiver.

"Let's *actually* get cleaned up," I suggest.

Denver yawns and nods as he reaches for the soap so we can finish our shower.

As soon as we're clean and dry, we climb into the bed, coming together again to hold each other close.

It's only been a few weeks, but I want to tell Denver I love him. Instead, I simply kiss his head, keeping the words to myself. We were supposed to take this slow, and we haven't been doing that. I'm afraid if I tell him how I feel, it will be too much and cause him to put distance between us.

And that's the last thing I want.

Chapter Nineteen

FORD

A LOUD BANG RINGS from my captain's office before he storms out with a red face, his hands clenched in tight fists at his side. He looks like he's ready to kill someone.

"They found another body," he growls out, and a shudder of ice runs down my spine before it turns to fire as the anger inside me builds.

"We need to catch this sick fuck *now*," Melody says through a clenched jaw, snapping the pencil she was holding.

"I feel the same way," Captain Gregory O'Connol tells her. "Whatever you need, let me know."

"Thanks, Cap," I say, grabbing my coat and heading out to examine the crime scene with Melody.

The drive to where the body was found doesn't take us long, and neither Melody nor I speak, our tempers simmering just below the surface.

"Do we have an ID on the victim?" Melody asks when we approach the officers who have secured the scene.

Thankfully, I've met both of these men before and know they wouldn't have fucked anything up. Not everyone is good at keeping everything exactly how it was.

Officer Carter shakes his head and grabs the back of his neck. "She didn't have anything on her. We're waiting for her picture to get run through the database to see if she was reported missing."

"Two young women found her while out for their morning run," Officer Maxwell supplies with a tilt of his head to the mentioned women speaking with Officer Oliver.

"I'll get their statements," Melody tells me before walking away.

"How bad is it?" I ask, not caring who responds.

"It's bad," Officer Carter groans.

I can only imagine how this is making him feel. He has two young daughters, and I bet this is hitting a little too close to home for him.

I walk toward the body covered in a white sheet and take a deep breath before reaching into my pocket, pulling out a pair of gloves, and putting them on. Carefully, I lift the sheet to not expose the body to lingering bystanders. My heart falls at the sight of the young girl, naked and bruised, with a number three carved into her chest. I quickly cover her again and stand to scan the area.

The body was found on a well-used walking trail, not even in the trees. The killer wanted her to be found.

My head throbs as I take in the scene. Honestly, not much looks out of place. It's obvious this was only a dumping ground. While I'm not a coroner, I'm pretty sure the young girl has been dead for at least a day or two.

Feet crunch on the gravel, and when I turn, I'm not surprised to find Melody making her way to me.

"The coroner just showed up," she informs me.

"I'm finding nothing here. It's obviously a dumping ground," I supply.

"Figured as much," she mutters with a sigh. "The women didn't see anything. Who knows how long the girl was here before they ran by."

"We have to figure out this fuckhead's motive," I grumble. "He clearly isn't trying to keep his kills a secret. He wants us to know what he's doing. There has to be something that connects these girls. Serial killers like this never do it randomly."

"Hopefully, we'll get a hit on who this girl is and be able to connect the dots. Three girls give us more to go on."

She isn't wrong, but it also sucks. *How many more girls have to die before we catch this sicko?*

I follow her to my car with a heavy heart. So far, the two girls we've been working on aren't matching up at all. One was thirteen, the other fourteen. One was a blonde with blue eyes, the other a brunette with hazel eyes. They went to different schools, had no friends in common, and had completely different tastes in activities.

Heather was into drama, dance, and makeup and loved to be out with her friends. Stefanie was a video gamer and more introverted.

I have a tight grip on the steering wheel as we make our way to the office. This feeling that we're missing something tingles in the base of my skull.

"I'm going to run through Heather and Stefanie's files again," I tell Melody as we walk to our desks.

"Knock yourself out. I'll let you know once we get an ID on the new vic."

With a sigh, I pick up Heather's file, rereading all the details we have gotten from research and interviewing everyone close to her. I'm not sure how many times I've been through this file now, but something has to connect her to Stefanie and the new victim.

"We've got a name," Melody calls out, pulling me from my focused state.

"Have the parents been informed?"

She nods, picking up her coffee cup and heading to refill it. "They're coming in shortly for us to interview."

I blow out a breath and run my hand over my face. I hate this part of the job. Who wants to poke and prod at the wounds of these people? They lost their child, and unless one of the parents was the serial killer, they had nothing to do with this. But they will be blaming themselves, nonetheless.

"Send me what we've got so far," I request once Melody is back at her desk, wanting to be as prepared for this interview as possible.

Shilo Davis

Fifteen

Westmore All Girls Academy

Parents still together

Above-average household income

"I'm calling the school to see if we can set up an interview with her teachers, principal, and maybe even her close friends," I tell Melody, who gives me a small smile.

"Sounds good. She's got a pretty big social media presence," she informs me.

Her words make something click inside my head.

"Does she have a YouTube channel?" I check.

"Yup, ten thousand followers. She talks about books."

"Heather had a makeup channel, and Stefanie had one about gaming," I supply.

"You think that's the connection?" she asks.

I shrug. "That's all I've got right now. Is there any way to figure out people who followed all three accounts?"

"We'll have to gain access to their accounts, but I think it's a possibility," she says.

"Get ahold of Heather and Stefanie's parents and request access. We can ask Shilo's parents after the interview is over."

"On it," Melody assures me, and we both get back to work.

It's looking to be another long day. I'm not even sure I'm going to get home on time for dinner tonight.

Pulling out my phone, I shoot off a quick text to Denver, letting him know today is turning out to be a shit show, and I'll be home late.

I hate having to miss even *more* time with him and Sammy, but that's the line of work I'm in.

It's dark outside when I walk inside, but I smile when I find Denver and his mom chatting on the couch.

"How was work?" Denver asks as I kick off my shoes.

"Tiring," I mutter. "I'll be right back." I head to the bedroom to change and secure my gun.

"Dinner's in the fridge," Mama Rachel tells me. "I'll warm it up for you."

I shake my head, waving for her to sit back down. "I'm an adult. I can warm my own food up," I assure her.

She giggles and settles onto the couch again.

After the leftovers are warm, I eat at the table. I'm not surprised when both Denver and his mom join me.

"Tell me about your day," I say before taking a big bite and moaning around the mouthful. "Damn, this is good."

Denver chuckles and rubs my back. "Did you eat lunch today?" he asks with a stern look that's so fucking hot.

"I had a sandwich, a few protein bars, and lots of coffee. That counts, right?" I tease, resulting in an eye roll from my handsome man.

"I guess that will have to do."

"Thanks for caring about me," I whisper, then kiss his cheek.

Denver blushes a little, which is sexy on him, and gives my shoulder a playful shove.

I chuckle and eat as they fill me in on their day. It sounds like a blast, and I can't help feeling a little bit jealous. I've always loved being a detective, but maybe I need a new line of work. Something that is going to allow me to be with my family more. And something that isn't so dangerous.

All I know is I don't want to miss out on everything, and I don't want to put my life on the line every time I walk out the door. I have a son now and a man I'm crazy about.

Maybe it's time for something else.

Chapter Twenty

DENVER

THE INTERNET SUCKS.

How is it that someone can post something and be a fucking ghost at the same time?

Both Ford and I are dealing with a similar issue in our careers. He's trying to find a serial killer they think is finding his victims through YouTube, and I'm working with my team to find Emilia's stalker.

"Find anything new?" I ask Sophy after a quick knock on her open door.

"Whoever this weirdo is knows a thing or two about being a ghost, which isn't your typical stalker," she informs me.

I groan, grabbing at the back of my neck. "Isn't that just great?"

"Has she received any more gifts?" she asks me, and I shake my head.

It's been a week since we've taken Emelia on as a client, and the stalker has become quiet, which isn't unheard of. Often, when someone hires full-time protection, stalkers will back off because the victim is harder to get to. However, that doesn't mean it's safe for her to let us go.

"Her social media has also quieted down. I mean, no more creepy comments or messages," she clarifies.

"Keep me in the loop if that changes," I request, then head to the front to spy on Sammy.

"He's fine," Margert tells me without even looking up from her computer.

She is currently typing with one hand and holding Sammy with the other. Mr. Man is batting at her necklace, both looking perfectly content.

"Well, if you need me, you know where I'll be," I say, heading to my office.

Who knew I would be jealous of my coworkers for helping me out? I want to be the one who cuddles Sammy all day, but I'm not as talented at multitasking as Margret, Sophy, or my mom. It must be a woman's superpower.

My phone rings as I'm about to sit down, Knox's picture popping up.

"What's up?" I answer.

"We're thinking about this all wrong," he starts, and I plop down in my chair, ready to hear his thoughts.

"Go on," I encourage him when he doesn't continue right away.

"What if the stalker is using the burner accounts to lead us on a wild-goose chase but is actually connecting with Emelia in other ways," he suggests.

"Like how?" I inquire, not quite following.

"What if the stalker is using a female account to become close with her? Build a connection that way?"

"Do you have any suspicions?" I check.

"GraceyLouLovesYouEightyNine," he rattles off the username, and I rush back to Sophy's office.

"Can you please pull up all the messages between Emelia and GraceyLouLovesYouEightyNine?"

She nods, fingers flying across her keyboard, making a loud clickety-clack noise as she goes.

Moving beside Sophy, I lean down, resting my hands on the edge of her desk, and read the messages. They all seem innocent, but Knox might be onto something.

"She wanted to meet for lunch yesterday but didn't show," Knox says, yet I don't see anything about it in the message thread.

"Are they talking on other apps?"

"They've been talking on WhatsApp," he supplies.

"Have they ever met in person before?"

"They've tried, but Emelia's schedule had been hectic. It would explain how the stalker knew where Emelia was going to be all the time. Gracey and her talk almost every day. Gracey's really the only person who knows all the ins and outs of Emelia's life."

"I'll dig into the account and see if I can find anything," Sophy tells me.

"What excuse did Gracey give for not showing up for lunch?" I ask Knox, wondering if that's what put him on alert.

"Emelia told her I would be there, then Gracey said she forgot about a doctor's appointment."

That's fishy.

"What does Emelia think about all of this?" I question.

"She doesn't think it can be Gracey, but it's our best lead for now."

"Have they ever video chatted or talked on the phone?" I ask.

"A few times, but apparently, Gracey's camera always stays off when they video chat."

"We'll look into it on our end. You let me know if you come up with anything else," I instruct.

Knox agrees, ending the call.

"Gracey sure follows a lot of young girls on social media," Sophy mutters.

I stare at the screen as she's scrolling through who Gracey is following on Instagram.

"Stop," I call out suddenly when a name I recognize pops up.

"What?" Sophy asks, looking confused.

"ShiloLovesBooks," I say, pointing to the screen. "Click on that account, please."

Sophy does and gasps when she realizes who it is. "It's one of the girls who is linked with the serial killer," she murmurs, and I nod.

I'm not supposed to know some of what I do, but the news outlets have gotten the police captain to admit there is a serial killer on the loose. Other than the knowledge that the person is targeting young girls, there isn't much information out there. The public isn't aware that the detectives believe the creep is finding his victims through YouTube.

I hastily scroll through my phone and call Ford. "What are the usernames for Heather and Stefanie?" I ask him as soon as he answers.

"Um... why?" he questions.

"I think we might have stumbled upon something. Please give me the usernames so I can figure out if I'm right."

I put the phone on speaker so Sophy can start typing as soon as he speaks.

"GlamItUpWithHeather," he tells us, and Sophy quickly searches for the username under Gracey's following list. When the account pops up, my blood runs cold.

"And the next," I coach, my voice quivering a little.

"GaminWithStef," he says.

Again, Gracey is following the account.

"Can I meet with you in twenty minutes to go over what we've found?" I inquire.

"Sure, I'll let Melody know you're on your way," he says, and we end the call.

"Holy shit," Sophy whispers. "Did we just find the serial killer?"

I take a shaky breath as I grab the back of my neck. "I'm not sure, but it's one hell of a coincidence if it's not."

As I'm heading out of the office, I pause and turn to Sophy. "Let Knox know to keep a close eye on their conversations, but don't inform him of the connection just yet. He'll want to cut off all ties, and I'm not sure we want that yet."

As soon as Sophy nods, I rush to the front.

"I'm taking Sammy for a road trip," I tell Margret as I pick him up from where he was enjoying some tummy time.

"He'll probably sleep in the car for you. Just make sure you change his diaper quickly before you leave."

I thank her and head to my office to change Sammy quickly before getting him comfortable in his car seat.

"Let's go see Daddy," I tell him with a quick kiss on his forehead.

The traffic is light as I drive to the precinct, but the energy running through my veins is a palpable vibration.

Never in a million years did I think the two cases we were working on would be connected like this. I know it is a long shot, but it's something.

"Oh my goodness, he's so cute," Gwendolyn, one of the receptionists at the precinct, says when I walk in with Sammy, who is fast asleep.

"Isn't he, though?" I respond with a smile. "We're here to see Ford. He's expecting us."

"Twenty minutes on the dot," Ford notes, appearing behind Gwen.

"I'm always on time," I tease and wave at Gwen before following Ford to a room where Melody is waiting for us, her laptop set up in front of her.

"Oh my goodness, I wish I could hold him," Melody coos.

"Maybe he'll wake up before we leave," I say, and her smile grows.

"So, what connection did you make?" Ford asks, getting us back on track.

"Our office is currently helping a client who has a stalker, and we've been trying to figure out who the person is. As you are all aware, sometimes finding people on the internet is harder than finding ghosts. But we found one person who started giving us red flags. When we were searching through their Instagram account, we found that they were also following all three of the murdered girls."

Melody's eyes go wide. "What is their username?" she requests, and I rattle off Gracey's handle.

She's silent as she checks accounts and messages.

"It looks like the account of a teenage girl," Ford says, looking over Melody's shoulder.

I nod. "Whoever is behind the account makes it look real, but I'm beginning to have my doubts."

"What started making you look into this account?" Melody asks, but her eyes stay glued on her screen.

"Knox's gut. Our client has been talking with this girl for two years and, in a way, has become close friends with her. She's one of the only people who knows our client's schedule as well as our client does. They text every day and have had a few phone and video calls, but Gracey's camera always stays off during those ones..." I pause as my head throbs from the possibility of all of this. "The other thing was they were supposed to meet up for lunch yesterday, but when our client told Gracey that she would be bringing her bodyguard, she bailed with the excuse of a forgotten appointment."

Melody pauses her scrolling. "This account is one we checked when we started making the social media connection, but we wrote it off as safe since none of the messages are threatening or concerning in any way. This Gracey person doesn't even ask any of the girls to meet."

"That you can tell," I add.

Melody sighs. "Both Heather and Stefanie's devices have been gone through with a fine-tooth comb, and nothing was found. We're still waiting to get Shilo's devices from the officers who were in charge of her missing person's case, but I doubt that will lead to anything. As far as this looks on our end, it's just a girl who has a wide interest in accounts reaching out to people she felt connected with. It wouldn't be enough to get a warrant to track locations."

I blow out a breath. I should have seen this coming. Their hands are tied, but mine aren't. We can still work this case from our end as long as it's under the guise of protecting Emelia.

"Thanks for bringing this to us anyway," Ford says. "We'll keep this account flagged for the time being and see if it leads us anywhere. It's something we could ask the parents about as well."

Sammy stirs, pulling our attention to something happier.

"Would you like to feed him his bottle?" I ask Melody.

Her face lights up. "Absolutely."

I free Sammy from his car seat and hand him to Ford first. "You can be a good Daddy and change his diaper," I tease.

He rolls his eyes at me but doesn't appear pissed. In contrast, I actually think he's happy to have a moment with his son. The way his eyes light up when Sammy smiles at seeing him makes it obvious Ford misses Sammy more than he lets on.

Each day, when Ford comes home, I watch him with Sammy, and it breaks my heart to see the sadness there. He tries to hide it, but I know the fear of missing out is eating at him. So, he makes every second count of these short, stolen moments, even if it's changing his diaper.

I would change places with him in a heartbeat, but that's not an option, and my brain keeps coming up blank for a plausible solution.

And as long as he's a detective, this is how life is going to be.

Chapter Twenty-One

FORD

"How was the rest of your day?" I ask Denver after I've changed.

"Uneventful," he replies with an easy grin.

"Did your mom make it home all right?"

He nods while moving around the kitchen, getting supper ready. "She texted me a little while ago. Safe and sound at home, already spoiling her other grandbabies."

I chuckle, pulling him in for a kiss.

"I love that she thinks of Sammy as her grandbaby," I murmur against his lips.

"I'm starting to think of him as my son," he responds so quietly I almost miss the words.

I beam at him and kiss him again. "You should because he is."

His eyes light up, and he gives me a gentle shove. "Let me finish getting dinner ready. You can spend some time with our boy," he tells me.

A rush of contentment washes over me at his words. Who knew something so simple could sound so perfect?

"Hi, handsome," I coo at Sammy as I pick him up from the floor, where he's hanging out, looking content.

He smacks his lips at me, and my heart fills with my love for him. I've always wanted kids, but I never realized exactly how amazing it would be. Everything changed the second I held him in my arms.

It's crazy how fast he's growing.

And I hate that I'm missing it.

"What would you think about me changing careers?" I ask Denver but keep my eyes on our son.

"What would you want to do?" he responds, placing our plates on the table.

I shrug and set our handsome baby into his vibrating bouncy chair. "I'm honestly not sure, but I hate how much I'm missing of Sammy's life. I know not all cases are this crazy, but I just don't think I can continue doing this line of work."

Denver puts his hand on my shoulder, giving me a gentle squeeze after I sit down. "I'll support you in whatever you decide to do, even if that's quitting after this case and taking some time to figure out what you want to do. I make enough money to support us, baby."

My chest tightens as the air gets trapped in my lungs.

"You'd do that?" I whisper.

Denver's warm smile sets me at ease as he rubs my shoulder. "I'd do anything for you. Always. Even if we weren't in a relationship. You're my best friend. All I ever want is for you to be happy."

I lean in for a gentle kiss. "I don't know what I did to deserve you."

"It's what best friends do. You'd do the same for me."

I nod, giving him another peck before sitting back. "Always."

I think this friendship is what I was always missing in previous relationships. Samantha and I were friends, but that wasn't the base of our relationship. We grew into that over the years. It's different starting things as friends and then moving into a romantic relationship.

"Would you like to try something new tonight?" I ask as we're cleaning up after dinner.

"What do you have in mind?" he questions with a raised brow and an amused smirk.

"I want to fuck you tonight," I tell him honestly.

He sucks in a breath of air and licks his lips. "That sounds amazing." His husky tone goes straight to my cock.

"I'll get Sammy down, then your ass is mine," I state before smashing my lips to his.

Denver is panting as I leave him with a smirk on my lips.

THE MAIN LIGHTS ARE off when I enter the bedroom, but a lamp on Denver's nightstand casts a soft glow over the space.

I strip out of my clothes before following the whooshing sound of the shower, more than ready to get my hands on my man.

"You're so sexy," I murmur after I pull the curtain back and step into the shower.

Denver chuckles and rolls his eyes, but a pleased grin is on his lips. "You're not so bad yourself," he tells me, letting his eyes roam up and down my body, taking in my naked state.

My half chub swiftly grows to a full erection when he stares at my cock, and this jolt of need runs down my spine.

With a steady step, I close the space between us, gripping his hips tightly and pressing my lips to his for a sensual kiss. It starts out slow, but when I buck my hips into Denver's, he growls, and the kiss turns heated. My tongue snakes its way into his mouth and dances with his as we make out passionately and grind against each other.

I'm so fucking hard it hurts when my man whimpers into my mouth. "I need you," he pleads, and even though I want him just as bad, I almost don't want to stop, but reluctantly, I take a step away.

"Let's clean up quickly, then. The first time my cock gets buried in your ass is not going to happen in the shower."

I almost laugh at how fast Denver grabs the soap and cleans his body. I do the same and smile at the extra attention he pays to his hole. I make a quick pass over my rock-hard cock but don't linger there. The anticipation alone would make it easy to blow, but there is no way I'm doing that until I'm balls deep inside my boyfriend. I only pray I won't be a two-pump chump.

Our lust-filled frenzy spurs us on, making it the quickest shower in history, and then we make our way to the bed.

"Kneel on the bed so I can stretch you," I command, opening the nightstand drawer and pulling out a bottle of lube.

Denver obeys me, climbing onto the bed and presenting his ass for me. My cock twitches, and a bead of precum leaks from the tip at the sight.

I don't move right away. Instead, I take a moment to soak this all in. Denver has never looked so hot. His upper back rises and falls with each heavy breath he takes, and his thick cock hangs heavy between his legs.

"What's taking so long?" he asks over his shoulder. His pupils are dilated, and his skin is flushed from the hot shower but also from need.

"Just admiring how fucking perfect you are," I whisper, pouring a dollop of lube onto my fingers and rubbing it in a little to warm them up.

My left hand rubs his ass, and his head falls as I press my index finger to his perfect pucker. The moan he releases as I slowly slide it in has my heart racing. I will never get sick of the noises he makes when we're fucking.

I take my time sliding my finger in and out of him and adjusting the angle in the right way to nail his prostate.

"Fuck," Denver mewls, his back bowing as I press firmly against it.

Since we've been using a dildo most nights, it doesn't take long before I'm able to add a second finger. I scissor them open, getting him ready to take me but also loving how fucking sexy he looks with my fingers in his ass.

Denver's needy cries get louder when I stick in a third finger. I'm dying to be inside him now, but he's not ready yet, and neither am I. This is a first for us, and I'm not going to rush anything.

"Need you," my sexy man begs, and I lean over to kiss his shoulder.

"Not yet," I whisper into his ear before pulling the lobe between my teeth. "We aren't in a rush. I want to make this so good for you."

I'm not as thick as Denver is, and he might be able to take me after only three fingers, but I want to see him take more.

"Jesus," he cries out as my pinky finger joins the others.

Denver's back bows again, and sexy, needy cries of pleasure leave his lips as I fuck him with four digits.

"Look at you taking this like a pro," I praise him. "You're so fucking hot. I can't wait to be buried balls deep inside you."

"Then... do it. Please... fuck me," he begs with heavy pants.

I pump my fingers into him a few more times before gingerly pulling them out.

Denver instantly cries out at the loss of my hand, and I bet he's feeling so empty right now, but I don't plan on leaving him like that for long.

"Flip over, baby," I instruct. "I want to see your face when I enter you."

He does as he's told, and I move for a condom. "I want to get tested," Denver says as I'm rolling it on.

All of a sudden, I'm flooded with the idea of filling him with my cum. I have to grip the base of my cock hard so I don't prematurely come. The thought alone is so fucking hot that it has me on the edge.

"I'd love to be bare with you," I tell him before taking a deep breath and licking my lips.

I'm careful not to linger long lubing my erection because that's how needy I am. I don't think I've ever wanted anything as bad as I want this. I also don't think I've ever been this turned on in my entire life.

Sex with Samantha was never like this.

With a firm tug, I bring Denver to the edge of the bed, press his knees to his chest, and line myself up with his entrance.

"Are you ready?" I check, making sure we're still on the same page.

"So ready. Please get inside me," he begs with lust-filled eyes.

With his go-ahead, I carefully push inside him. Denver's mouth falls open as he gasps, and my eyes roll into the back of my head.

"Jesus," I gasp out. "You feel amazing."

"Mmm is his response, which makes me smirk.

Denver is so tight and hot and perfect. As much as I'm strung out on lust and need right now, I also can't help but notice how perfect this moment feels. This is exactly where I'm meant to be, connected with the man who was made for me.

I rock my hips back and forth, carefully pumping in and out of him, getting a little deeper with each gentle thrust.

It's crazy how intense this feels. I've had anal sex before, but it—*this*—feels different. It's somehow *more*. Once I've bottomed out and my balls are resting against his body, I lean down to kiss Denver, giving him some time to adjust to my size and myself a second to keep it all together.

Three words are on the tip of my tongue, but I don't say them. I don't want the first time I tell him I love him to be in the heat of the moment. So instead, I deepen the kiss, smashing my lips into his and using my body to show him how I feel about him. The kiss is passionate, and we're left panting for air when we break.

"I need you to fuck me," Denver begs between breaths after a few minutes of making out.

"How do you want it?" I ask, wanting to make this perfect.

"I want to feel you, all of you. I need you to take me... hard," he pleads. "Don't hold back."

A shiver of anticipation runs down my spine, and I kiss him again before standing back up. With a few careful full strokes, I test to make sure there is no pull and enough lube. The last thing I want to do is hurt my man.

Once I'm certain everything is perfect, I look into Denver's eyes and see he's already a blissed-out mess, so I pull my hips back and slam into him. A beautiful cry of pleasure releases from Denver, egging me on. His moans of ecstasy push at me, driving me to completely let go and lose control, so I do.

I fuck him with everything I have. Grabbing onto his muscled thighs, I spread him wider for me. Leaning into him more, I bury my cock inside, over and over again. His tight little ring, now stretched around me, glides up and down my shaft, milking my flesh and urging my release closer. But I won't give in. Not yet. I can't. This feels too good, and I don't ever want it to end.

I take him hard and fast, drilling myself into him, wild and un-leashed. My desperation for him echoes back at me from his glazed eyes.

I'm barely holding on when I reach down for his leaking cock. Using his precum, I jack him off, matching the rhythm of my fist to my pounding thrusts into his ass.

We are both panting hard with sweat coating and dripping down our bodies. This primal need is in complete control of us as we connect in this most basic of ways.

"So fucking good," Denver cries out.

His words cause a tingle to form at the base of my spine, a telltale sign that I'm about to come.

"Please, are you close?" I ask, wanting my man to lose it at the same time as me.

He nods, panting and moaning when I shift my hips to nail his prostate with each hard thrust.

"That's it, baby. Let go. Come for me," I demand as I bring a last burst of speed to my fist and hips.

"Oh shit," Denver screams, his cock releasing his warm cum like a fountain.

His already tight channel clenches around me, pulling me over the edge with him. I gasp for air as I release into the condom, wishing it was him I was filling.

I've never had an orgasm this intense in my entire life. It feels like I'm coming forever, and it leaves me a little lightheaded.

"Damn," I murmur, falling forward, barely catching myself on my forearms.

We both take some time to recover, and part of me never wants to pull out. Being inside Denver is the best thing I've ever felt, and I don't want to let that go.

"We're perfect together," I whisper once I feel like I can talk again, then pepper my man's face with gentle kisses.

"I think you just fucked me stupid," he murmurs. I chuckle, and Denver wiggles. "That's weird, I can feel you when you laugh."

I smile and hold my man for a little while longer before reluctantly pulling out as my cock softens.

My legs feel like I'm walking on Jell-O as I head to the bathroom, where I ditch the condom and give my dick a quick cleaning. Then I grab a washcloth and return to the room, where Denver appears to have melted into the mattress in bliss.

"Let me clean you up," I tell him as I gently clean the cum from his stomach, chest, and cock. His body shivers when I touch his over-sensitive dick, so I make sure not to linger there. After his front is clean, I swipe the cloth between his legs, wiping his lubed pucker and cheeks.

"I'm a lucky man," he replies, and I smirk.

Satisfied that he's clean enough, I toss the cloth toward the hamper, not caring if it lands inside.

"I think I'm going to sleep amazing tonight," Denver mumbles as we climb into bed together. His head finds a place on my chest, and I realize nothing has ever felt this good.

Denver is my person. I'm never letting him go.

Chapter Twenty-Two

FORD

"You look extra happy this morning," Melody notes as I walk into the office.

I shrug, but the grin on my face never falls. "Had a good night."

"Are you seeing someone?" she asks with narrowed eyes.

Denver and I haven't had time to plan a games night like we originally talked about, so I decide now is as good of a time as any to tell Melody what's going on. I refuse to lie to her or hide what's happening with my best friend and me.

"Denver and I are dating now," I tell her, wringing my hands in front of me, hoping her response is good.

She beams at me and claps her hands, and the tiny bit of tension building in my shoulders releases. "That's amazing. I'm so happy for you."

"Thanks, things are going really well," I say as I pour myself a cup of coffee. "Did Shilo's devices show up?" I turn the conversation back to work, even though I'd rather not.

Melody nods as Carson, one of our cyber techs, rushes into the room.

"I've found something," he huffs out as he tries to catch his breath.

"Did you run here?" I question with a raised brow.

"It's important," he replies.

"Well..." Melody urges, rolling her hand for him to continue.

"I think Gracey's account needs to be looked at more closely. I found another missing social media star."

I blow out a breath. "How old?"

"Eighteen. Her best friend filed the missing person report. It doesn't look like the officers who were assigned the case have been taking it seriously. She's run away before," he grumbles.

"We have to tell Captain," Melody states.

I tilt my head toward the captain's office. "Come on."

"Hey, Cap, Carson found another missing person that should be added to our caseload," I state after he tells us to come in.

"How long has she been missing?" he barks at Carson, who shudders next to me.

"About a week. The missing person case was only filed a few days ago, but the person who reported it says it's been longer," Carson replies, still shaking.

"Get me the details. I'll get the case assigned over to you," the captain responds.

"Thanks, Cap, but this also links another person to the Gracey account we had an alert put on," I add.

"That should be enough for us to request a subpoena to track the IP address and get the information they submitted on the back end of their social media accounts. I want to know who this person is. Carson, in the meantime, find everything you can on this account."

Carson nods rapidly like a little nerdy bobblehead. "Yes, sir," he murmurs.

"We'll go interview the friend," Melody tells the captain, who nods in response.

"Go. I'll get to work on the warrant. We need to catch this fucker yesterday."

We do as we're told and leave his office.

"Send us the details for the friend, please," I request of Carson.

"On it," he assures us, then rushes to his office.

Once the details are in our inbox, we make our way to the apartment of the friend.

"Cynthia O'Hanna?" Melody asks after the door is opened.

She nods but doesn't speak.

"I'm Detective Daniels, and this is my partner, Detective Lynol," I tell her, holding out my badge. "We wanted to ask you some questions about your friend, Vanessa Rubble."

"Okay," she says and steps aside to let us in.

"She *didn't* run away" is the first thing Cynthia tells us once we're seated in her living room. "She wouldn't ghost me like this."

"Can you tell us more about the day she went missing?" Melody requests with a kind smile.

"We were both working at the strip club that night, but I rolled my ankle and had to cut my shift early," Cynthia explains. "I told Nessa I'd wait for her, but she wouldn't hear of it. Insisted I head home to take care of myself. I didn't think I had anything to worry about, so I agreed. When I got home, I took a couple of extra-strength painkillers that knocked me out. It was morning when I finally woke up. She wasn't here. I called her cell, but it went straight to voicemail, which is unusual since she never shuts her phone off and charges it while we're at the club. I tried a few more times before calling another girl who was working with us. She said she saw Nessa get in a cab but hasn't heard from her since..." She pauses, taking a shaky breath. "I'm scared. I think something bad happened."

"Do you have Vanessa's computer?" I ask.

"I do," she states and rushes to retrieve it.

"What club do you work at?" Melody inquires when Cynthia returns.

"Red Light District," Cynthia says. "My dancer name is Petal, and Nessa's is Trixie. We love where we work. It's a good place, and everyone is worried about Nessa. Please find her," she begs. "She's all I've got. We both grew up with shitty parents and don't have anyone else."

"We'll do all that we can," I tell her as honestly as possible. "If you think of anything else, please let us know."

"I will," she says and escorts us to the door.

"Care to join me at a strip club tonight?" Melody asks with a waggle of her brows.

"Let me just text Denver to let him know I won't be home until later."

"I should let Donny know too. Afterward, I'll call the club. Maybe they'll meet us before they open," she says, and I nod, pulling out my phone.

Me: *Might have a new lead, but I'll probably be home late tonight.*

Denver: *Sounds good. Stay safe.*

Me: *Always do. Especially now. I have two very important people waiting at home for me.*

Denver: *We'll wait as long as you need us to.*

I chuckle and pocket my phone.

"Any luck?" I ask Melody.

She shrugs. "I left a message. Fingers crossed, they'll call back. Come on, let's get this back to Carson," she says, grabbing the laptop.

My mind is racing as we get into the car and drive back to the precinct. My blood is also boiling. *Why can't we catch this fucker already? Why do more girls have to keep going missing?*

I grip the wheel tightly while focusing solely on the road and trying to calm my frustration.

The drive is quick, and we find Carson busy typing away when we return, so I knock on his office door.

"Find anything on the Gracey account?" I ask after Carson waves us in.

He sighs and shakes his head. "Whoever this is... they're good. Once the subpoena arrives, I'll start tracking the IP address, but I have a sinking suspicion that won't be easy. They are covering their tracks as much as possible. I highly doubt they will be using one location for all of this. I bet all of the locations are going to be places like coffee shops and libraries. They won't be doing it from their home, which will require more subpoenas to gain access to security cameras. It's gonna be a long game. Even then, we don't exactly know who we're looking for yet."

"What if Gracey talks with someone regularly? Don't you think they would do that from their house?" I question.

Carson tilts his head to the side. "Probably, but they also most likely use a VPN..." He pauses, studying me. "Do you know someone who talks to Gracey regularly?"

I nod. "I have to talk to Cap first, but if we get the green light from him, this could be the break we were looking for."

Carson waves his hands at us. "What are you waiting for? Go."

Melody and I rush out of Carson's office toward our captain's. I pray he agrees to work with Hunter Security and their client. I also hope the client is willing to help us out.

Chapter Twenty-Three

DENVER

My screen turns blurry as I stare at it while sorting through a few new client request forms.

"You've got a visitor," Margret says through the intercom system.

Instead of responding, I stand and make my way to the front.

My eyes go wide when they land on Ford. "I thought you were working late tonight?"

He doesn't respond right away, and he's worrying his lower lip between his teeth. Then my eyes land on Melody standing behind him.

My brows pinch together as I try to figure out why they are here. It's obvious this isn't a friendly visit.

"What brings you guys in?" I inquire.

"Can we talk in your office?" Ford requests with his lips turned down, and his shoulders slumped.

I can tell something is weighing heavily on him. I'm almost certain it has to be the case. If they are here, it probably means they are taking the Gracey account more seriously.

I guide Melody and Ford to my office, shutting the door behind us.

"What's up?" I ask, heading to my chair and sitting down as they do the same on the other side of my desk.

"Would your client who has connections with the Gracey account be willing to help us out?" Ford questions.

I was right, but I'm not sure what they want Emelia to do. I can't endanger our clients, even if it means helping my boyfriend.

"What do you have in mind?"

"We would like for her to come to the precinct and message Gracey while we try and get a lock on the IP address. Gracey might be using a VPN, which would be trickier, but either way, this will give us more information than we currently have," Melody states.

I take a pause before responding, calculating the risk factor of the task. Messaging Gracey while in the presence of great officers isn't particularly dangerous. And since they talk often, it wouldn't feel out of place or clue Gracey in to what's happening. The last thing I would want is for Gracey to lash out at Emelia. Obviously, she has a bodyguard with her twenty-four seven, but putting my team at risk isn't something I'm too keen on.

"When would you like to do this?" I ask after I think it through.

"As soon as possible. We have another missing girl. Time is of the essence," Ford replies and sighs.

Shit, I feel so bad for him. This case is eating at him. I want to help out as much as I can.

"Let me call Knox. I'll see if Emelia would be up for it," I tell them, picking up the phone and dialing.

"What's up?" Knox answers.

"Ford and his partner Melody are here at the office asking for Emelia to help them with their case," I inform him.

"What do they want?" he grumbles.

I almost laugh at how protective he gets of nearly all his clients.

"They want Emelia to join them at the precinct as soon as possible and message Gracey. They will be tracing the IP address. This account is a suspect in their case."

"What if they don't find Gracey and whoever is behind the account clues in that Emelia was the one who helped the cops?" he asks the same question that was floating around my head.

"It's a risk, but I think it's a low one," I state. "They are willing to work around Emelia's schedule, but the sooner, the better."

"Give me a second."

I wait patiently as he talks to Emelia. With the line silent, I turn my gaze to Ford, who is stressed. I wish I could relieve the tension he's carrying between his shoulders.

"Does tonight work?" Knox asks when he comes back.

I pull the receiver away from my head. "Is tonight too soon for your team?"

Ford shakes his head. "We'll make it work," he assures me. "We have a few things we'll have to sort out, but as soon as we have a time, I can let you know."

I bring the receiver back to my ear and tell him, "Tonight works. I'll let you know the time soon."

He grunts out a response, acknowledging he heard me, and ends the call.

"Thank you for this," Melody says as we stand.

"Hopefully, this helps you catch the sicko," I state.

She nods before leaving my office.

"I don't think I'll be home too late anymore," Ford says, stepping toward me to give me a brief kiss. "We've arranged a time tomorrow to meet with the strip club owner to discuss the missing girl. Emelia's message will help us, but we'll still need more subpoenas if Gracey is using a VPN, which we won't be able to get until tomorrow."

I nod and hold him for a minute before I pull away, then follow him to the front, where he pauses to kiss Sammy on the head, gives me a smile, and leaves.

I pray they catch the guy and nothing crazy happens in the process.

THE MOMENT FORD WALKS through the door, I head to him and pull him into my arms.

"How did everything go?"

"As suspected, Gracey is using a VPN. But we now know which company is being used and will have a subpoena to get the IP address tomorrow morning. That will help us narrow down the location and get this asshole."

"Good," I say, holding him tightly. "So tomorrow might be a crazy day?"

He sighs and rubs my back. "Probably. I just want this case to be over already. I hate that these missing girls keep turning up dead."

We don't let go for a while. It's only when Sammy makes a noise that we separate.

"Come on, let's take care of our boy. Then we can eat and spend the night cuddling," I suggest with a tilt of my head.

"How 'bout more than cuddling?" he asks with a waggle of his brows that has me chuckling.

"I thought you'd be too tired after a busy day," I tease.

He places his large hands on my hips and pulls me into his solid chest, the lips of my best friend landing on mine. "Maybe it's because this is still so new, or maybe it's just you, but I don't think I'll ever be too tired to want you."

I give him a gentle shove before making my way to the kitchen. "I guess some sexy times can be arranged for later," I tell him over my shoulder.

The way his face lights up fills my chest with this warm, gooey feeling.

I'm already in love with Ford, but I'm afraid to just come out and say it. I worry it's too soon, but maybe it isn't. I guess I'm just waiting for the time to feel... I don't know... right.

Chapter Twenty-Four

FORD

THE SECOND THE SUBPOENA is in, Carson gets to work on getting the information we need to find Gracey.

"Got you," Carson says with a giant grin after who knows how long passes.

"Get the cap," I tell Melody, and she nods and rushes to his office.

"What did you find?" the captain asks Carson.

"The IP address is registered to a Brandon Amaro. He was in the northern part of the city last night when he was talking with Emelia," Carson says timidly.

I'm pretty sure he's intimidated by the captain.

"Okay, I'll get the DA to request a warrant to search the property so we can bring Brandon in for questioning. I'll also try for another subpoena to gain the GPS data for his cell phone. Let's set up a team and get ready. Keep working on getting us as much information on Brandon as possible," the captain says to Carson.

With that, the captain leaves to get things rolling.

"I'll be right back," I say to Melody, then go outside and call Denver.

"How's it going, handsome?" he answers.

His voice has a way of calming me and brings a small smile to my lips. "We've got a possible name and location. We'll be heading in once all the paperwork is in order," I tell him.

"Be careful," he pleads.

"I will be. I've got my world waiting at home for me."

"You do, and we love you," Denver whispers.

My heart skips a beat, and for a second, it's hard to breathe.

"You love me?" I ask, my voice wobbling with emotion.

"I do, so make sure you catch this prick and get home to me and our baby."

"I love you too, and I promise I'll see you in a little bit," I tell him, trying to sound as certain as possible.

We both stay silent for a moment, and I need to get back inside even though I don't want to end the call.

"I should get going. I love you," I tell him again.

"Love you too," he responds, then ends the call.

I didn't want the first time we said those words to be over the phone, but I'm glad we said them.

It's LATE AFTERNOON BY the time we have all the paperwork we need, a location, and a team ready to go. Melody and I are in our tactical gear, leading a small team around the back of a small house in a quiet neighborhood.

The chances of Vanessa being here are low, but I'm still trying to keep my hopes up.

We are quiet as we enter the house, using hand signals to communicate. Once the main floor is cleared, we head to the basement, where we find a man typing away on a computer. He's a skinny man with dark, greasy hair and matches the pictures we discovered of Brandon.

"Hands up," I shout with my gun aimed at his head.

"You finally found me," he says with an evil smirk, but he doesn't move.

"I said, hands up," I repeat, taking a few steps closer to him. "You're under arrest."

I'm now standing more in the middle of the room while my team lines up behind me and along the walls. Melody sneaks down the hall to see if she can find Vanessa.

"It's such a shame that our games have to end," he says with a sigh.

"Get your fucking hands up," I yell.

Brandon laughs and shakes his head. "What fun would that be? I mean, I *could* listen to you, or I could take you all down with me."

I don't have time to comprehend his words or react before his hand moves, and he hits a button that causes explosives to go off from within the walls. The sound is deafening, and the house collapses before I have time to process what's happening.

Something hits me in the head, and the world goes dark.

Chapter Twenty-Five

DENVER

On my way to the hospital with Sammy in the back seat, dead asleep, I'm numb. It's been this way ever since I got the phone call that rocked my world right before nap time.

I don't have details as of yet. All I know is Ford is at the hospital, and I need to get there as soon as possible.

Once I've found a parking spot, I grab Sammy from the back seat and head to the front desk.

"I'm looking for Ford Daniels. My name is Denver London. I got a call that he was here," I tell the older lady.

She keeps typing away for a few seconds before nodding. "If you'll just have a seat, someone will be out to talk to you shortly," she says with a warm smile.

I turn to find an empty seat when my eyes land on Ford's boss. "Captain O'Connol," I call out, making my way to him. "What happened?"

Captain O'Connol shakes his head, staring at his feet. "It was a fucking shit show." He runs his hands through his hair. It's then I notice he's shaking. "The sick fucker had the house rigged to explode at the push of a button."

I gasp, covering my mouth with my free hand.

"Ford?" I whisper, not being able to say more than that.

Captain O'Connol shakes his head again as I fight back a sob. "He was alive when he left the scene, but I don't know more than that," he says, sounding defeated. "If you'll excuse me, I have to talk to the families of those who didn't make it. I'll touch base with you later."

I nod as he walks away and find a chair to wait in. I'm thankful that since my mom moved away, Ford and I have listed each other as emergency contacts. It means the doctor will be able to tell me what's going on as soon as they know.

There is a television on the wall playing some do-it-yourself show, and even though I'm staring at it, I'm not watching. My thoughts keep drifting to my man. He's been my ride-or-die almost my entire life, and now he might not be in my life at all anymore.

"Mr. London?" a younger woman with a bright smile calls out.

Standing, I grab Sammy's car seat and follow the woman to a beige room.

"The doctor will be in shortly," she tells me. My stomach knots as I sit in a stiff chair.

Is this when they tell me that they're sorry for my loss? Why can't they just bring me right to Ford's room?

I'm not sure how much time passes before a soft rap on the door pulls my attention and an older woman in a white coat enters the room.

"Hi, Mr. London. I'm Dr. Ledger," she greets, taking a seat across from me. I nod, not sure what to say. "You were listed as Mr. Daniels's emergency contact," she starts.

"Yes, he's my boyfriend," I tell her.

"He was brought in today in critical condition and rushed into surgery immediately. He experienced a traumatic brain injury, and there was bleeding on the brain that we had to stop. Along with that, his left arm was broken in several places. We had to put pins in to stabilize the fracture..." She pauses, and I take in a shaky breath.

"Is... is he alive?" I stammer out, tasting something salty on my tongue.

Shit, I'm crying, and I didn't even realize it. That's how numb I am right now.

"He is, but he isn't out of the woods yet. He is in a medically induced coma for now. We are waiting for the swelling of his brain to come down. The next few days will be very telling. For now, we just have to wait and be patient. The body can do amazing things, and he is in good hands here, but it's too soon to give absolutes."

"Can I see him?" I ask, my voice wobbling as I force the words out.

"You can, but I'd just like to prepare you for what you'll see. As I already told you, Mr. Daniels is in a coma, so he won't be able to communicate with you, but what you're about to see might not be easy on you. He's covered in bruises, cuts, scratches, and even some burns. He's attached to a lot of equipment to monitor his state and provide him with what he needs while he's in the coma. Sometimes it's triggering for family members to witness their loved ones in a state like that, and it's completely okay to want to avoid seeing him for some time. No one will judge you for that," she assures me.

I shake my head. "No, I want to see him, please."

"Okay," she says and stands. "I'm sorry, but the baby is not allowed into the ICU. We can stop at the front to see if a nurse is free to spend a little time with him in the waiting room."

I nod and pick up Sammy. Once he's in the capable hands of a friendly nurse, I follow the doctor down a long hallway, my heart racing with every step.

"Be mindful not to touch any of the monitors or lines," Dr. Ledger tells me when we stop outside a room. "You can talk to him, though.

We can't say for sure if patients in this state can hear you or not, but it doesn't hurt to say some words of encouragement, even if it's just for you to hear." She squeezes my shoulder before walking away to let me have some alone time with Ford.

When I enter the room, I gasp at seeing my best friend and lover in such a fragile state.

Time almost feels like it's standing still as I make my way to his bed.

"Hi, handsome," I whisper through tears, grabbing a chair and pulling it beside the bed. Once I'm seated, I place a hand on Ford's arm, careful not to hit any wires. "You need to come back to me. I don't want to live this life without you," I tell him even though he's asleep. "I love you."

After a few deep breaths, I lean back in the chair, pull out my phone, and hit a button.

My entire body is shaking as the phone rings.

"Hello?" Mom answers, and a sob breaks past my lips as I let out all the emotions I've been keeping mostly locked up.

"We need you," I manage to choke out.

"I'm on my way," she assures me.

I'm not able to say more than a quick *I love you* before ending the call.

My body shakes heavily as I cry, praying to whatever deity will listen to bring my man back to me.

Lost in a brain fog, staring at Ford, I'm unaware of how much time has passed, but I'm sure Sammy needs me, so I reluctantly stand with tears still in my eyes.

"I've got to take Sammy home, but we'll be back soon," I tell Ford and kiss his head tenderly, making sure I'm applying as little pressure as possible. *I wish there weren't bandages in my way.*

More tears pool in my eyes as I head out of the room. I let the nurse watching Sammy know I'll be back tomorrow, and she assures me they'll call if there are any changes.

The last thing I want to do right now is leave the man who holds my heart, but our son needs me, and Ford would hate me if I didn't take good care of him.

When I get home from the hospital, I talk to my mom on the phone again, tell her everything that has happened, and cry some more. The tears seem to be endless.

Thankfully, my mom is able to get a flight out on short notice and will be here in the morning.

I'm trying to be the guy Sammy is used to, but even our innocent baby can tell something's off. As soon as I have him down for the night, I lie in bed, sobbing and feeling helpless. Hopeless.

I must have cried myself to sleep because I wake to Sammy's coos of hunger. I'm all out of tears, and I feel foggy now. My body is heavy, and the world is in black and white.

My body is on autopilot as I navigate life and take care of Sammy, but my mind is filled with all the what-ifs. What if Ford doesn't wake up? What if he wakes up but isn't the same person? What if I lose him?

Brain injuries aren't predictable, and that eats at me even more. I wish I had some answers to what the future will be like instead of being stuck in this stupid waiting game.

I don't have time to dwell as I take in the time. Mom will be arriving shortly, so after I feed and burp Sammy, I make sure he has a dry diaper on, and out the door we go.

The drive to the airport is a haze, thoughts of Ford on repeat. When we get to the pickup line, people pass by in a blur as we wait for my mom.

A knock on the window pulls me from my disconnection.

"You look like shit," my mom says as I get out to help her load her suitcase into the back of my SUV.

I shrug my shoulders, not having a response ready.

"Did you sleep at all?" she asks.

Again, I stay silent, letting my body language speak for me.

Mom lets out a long sigh and gets into the car. "You know you don't have to keep it all inside, right?"

I sigh as I pull away from the curb. "I'm just trying to keep my head above water, Mom. Sammy needs me. Nothing else matters right now," I respond after a long, awkward silence.

When I cast her a quick glance, I see her soft eyes filled with worry.

"Sammy needs you, but you can't care for him if you don't care for yourself," she reminds me.

I nod, still unable to formulate words that make any sense. She obviously isn't wrong, but how does one sleep when the person who is nearly their entire world is fighting for their life in a hospital bed?

"When we get home, you're going to take a nap, then you can go visit Ford," she commands in a tone that leaves no room for argument. "You aren't alone in this. Let me help."

Her words remind me of all the times I said that to Ford.

"Okay," I whisper.

There's no use in fighting. I'm going to drop dead if I don't get some rest.

I hope sleep will help bring a little color back to the world, but I know deep down it won't. The only thing that will make everything better is Ford waking up from that fucking coma.

Chapter Twenty-Six

DENVER

IT'S BEEN ONE MONTH since the explosion, and while Ford is no longer in a coma, he's not exactly awake either. The doctors and nurses call it a post-coma unresponsive state, which could last for *months*. It's a waiting game at this point, but it's driving me nuts.

"Hi, handsome," I greet Ford as I do every day when I visit. "You've got some new visitors coming today." I pull one of the chairs toward the bed. "Some of our friends have been worried sick."

It feels weird talking to someone who can't respond, but occasionally, his lashes will flutter or his finger will twitch. It gives me hope that he'll be coming back to me soon.

"Knock, knock," a deep voice calls out.

I look up to see Nixon and Dante standing in the doorway.

With a big smile, I stand and bring my dear friend in for a hug. "Sorry, I've kind of dropped the ball on my duties to fill your shoes this past month," I whisper.

Nixon shakes his head. "You've clearly had a lot going on. Turns out, we've built a strong team, and in a pinch, everyone comes together."

He isn't wrong. While my mom is still here helping out with Sammy, my coworkers have also been stopping by with casseroles and a listening ear, even offering to watch Sammy so Mom and I could visit at the same time. It's been a blessing.

"How's he doing?" Dante asks with an empathetic look.

I shrug. "He still hasn't woken up. No one knows how long it will take."

"Dante did a lot of research on Ford's condition on the flight over. I wish we could have come back sooner," Nixon tells me, but I wave him off.

"There's nothing you could have done, and everyone else has been more than supportive," I assure him.

He nods, and we all sit to visit. I'm happy to hear about the adventures they got up to in Brazil. It's nice to have my friend back, especially in such an uncertain time of my life.

Once Dante and Nixon leave, with promises to be back soon, I grab Ford's hand and squeeze it.

"Come back to me, baby. I miss you like crazy."

Chapter Twenty-Seven

FORD

THE SOFT SINGING OF a lullaby flutters through my ears, waking me from a tranquil sleep. Along with the peaceful song are rhythmic beeps and quiet chatter.

Now that I'm waking, I want to stretch my limbs but can't. I keep trying to move, but my body is not cooperating. My eyes won't even open, even though I'm putting all my focus into it.

What the fuck is happening? Why can't I move or open my eyes?

I'm beyond frustrated, but I don't want to give up. Finally, after much effort, I get my fingers to twitch, and I want to cheer with the small win, but that's obviously not possible.

"I think he's waking," a familiar and comforting voice says, but my brain feels foggy, refusing to tell me who it is.

"I'll get the doctor," someone else responds.

I wish I could open my goddamn eyes.

Doctor? Where the fuck am I?

Frustration is taking over. If I could scream right now, I would.

"I'm right here, baby," a man tells me, his hand gripping mine.

I recognize his voice but, again, can't put a name to it. All I know is the voice is calming my nerves.

I put all my focus into squeezing his hand back. I want to cry when my fingers finally move.

"He squeezed my hand," the man shouts, clear delight in his tone.

"The doctor is on her way. I'll just check his vitals," a woman says, probably speaking to the man still holding my hand.

Trying to siphon the strength from the man holding my hand, I attempt to open my eyes again. After what feels like forever, they finally slowly flutter open. The room I'm in is bright, so I squeeze them shut again as the hand in mine jolts.

"Take your time, baby," the man coaches.

I take a few deep breaths, listening to him before attempting to open my eyes again. This time, when they flutter open, I'm prepared for the bright lights, and slowly, the room comes into focus.

The handsome man holding my hand is the first thing my eyes land on. His eyes are bloodshot with dark bags underneath them like he hasn't slept in weeks. He's so familiar to me, and his smile is warm, but I still can't pinpoint how I know him.

"Hi, handsome," he whispers.

"Hi," I respond but immediately regret responding as my throat burns like a bitch.

"Can he have water?" a woman standing behind the man, holding a baby, asks.

"Absolutely," a different woman responds.

I turn to find who the voice belongs to. A blonde in bright pink scrubs walks away and returns with a cup and straw.

"Just take sips, Mr. Daniels," she says.

Is that my name? Why can't I remember my name?

The man takes the cup from her and brings the straw to my lips. As instructed, I sip the water. The cool liquid calms the burn, soothing my throat.

"It's good to see you awake," a woman in a white lab coat says, walking into the room. "I'm Dr. Ledger. How are you?" she asks.

I shrug, not sure I want to try responding.

"Do you know where you are?" she questions.

"Hospital?" I respond, and thankfully, it doesn't hurt as bad this time.

"That's correct," she says and makes a note.

"Can you tell me your name and date of birth?" she inquires.

I press my lips together, trying to find the information, but it won't come.

I slowly shake my head, and the woman holding the baby gasps. The doctor writes something else down in her notes.

"Do you know why you're here?" the doctor asks.

Again, I shake my head. "Why can't..." I start to ask, but it hurts again.

"Take your time," she encourages as the man brings the straw back to my lips, and I take some more sips.

"Why... why can't I remember anything?" I manage to squeak out.

"You were in an explosion. You were knocked in the head by debris from the building, which caused a traumatic brain injury. It isn't uncommon for people to experience some form of memory loss from an injury like that."

The man standing beside me is shaking as he holds my hand. Even though I can't remember who he is, I don't want him to let go. Something inside me is telling me he's safe, and I'm going to trust that.

I squeeze the man's hand and look at him with a small smile.

"Do you remember us?" he asks with a shaky voice, glancing at the woman holding the baby.

"I'm sorry, no. Your voice is familiar, and your presence calms me, but I don't know who you are."

Tears trickle down the woman's face, and the man's eyes become glassy with tears. Clearly, that wasn't the response they were hoping for.

"How long until I remember things again?" I ask the doctor.

The doctor shakes her head with her lips pressed together. "I'm sorry, I don't have the answer to that. You could start getting trickles of memories, or it could come all rushing back. It could take hours, days, weeks, months, or it could never come back. Every person is different."

"But the fact that my voice is familiar is promising, right?" the man questions.

"It's a positive for sure," she assures him. "What we should focus on is what we do know and hope the memory comes back when it's ready."

The urge to comfort him washes over me, but seeing as my muscles still feel heavy and don't want to move, there isn't much I can do.

"Along with your brain injury, you sustained a fracture of your left arm as well as some burns from the explosion and some scrapes and bruises. You were only in a coma for about a week but have been in a post-coma unresponsive state for almost two months, so most of your other injuries have already healed. You are actually scheduled to get your cast off today," the doctor tells me with a smile. "Now that you are awake and responsive, there is going to be lots of physical therapy since your body hasn't moved on its own in eight weeks. We'll also want you to be assessed by a psychiatrist, who could possibly help with your memory issues."

That makes me feel hopeful.

A noise pulls my attention from the doctor, and I realize it's the baby blowing bubbles.

As I stare at the handsome little man, my head throbs, and I close my eyes. Behind my lids is a vision of a woman lying in a hospital bed, holding my hand as she screams. Also beside me in the memory is the handsome man. The memory fades as another comes into play. I'm in a rocking chair, holding the baby, while the man stands behind me, grasping my shoulder and looking at us with love-filled eyes. The next memory is of the older woman who is here today playing with the baby, and finally, all their names and mine come back to me.

As I blink my eyes open, everyone is staring at me with concern written all over their faces.

"Are you okay?" Denver asks.

"I'm more than okay, baby," I tell him, then look at his mom. "Can you bring Sammy closer, Mama Rachel?"

"You remember," Denver says as Mama Rachel brings my son closer.

"Little man helped me," I whisper. "I still can't remember the explosion you were talking about," I tell the doctor.

"Like I said, everyone's memory loss is different. I'm just happy you are regaining some memories already."

She tells us a few more things before leaving, and I smile at my handsome man.

"I can't believe I've been away from you for so long," I tell both Denver and his mom. "Look how big Sammy has gotten."

"Babies grow fast," Mama Rachel says with a warm smile. "But we're just happy you're awake now."

"We've been taking good care of him, but I know he's happy to see you," Denver assures me.

"I can't wait to be able to hold him again." As the words leave my lips, another memory takes over. I squeeze my eyes shut as I remember why I'm in this hospital bed.

I gasp and open my eyes again.

"Are you okay?" Denver asks as I take a few deep breaths.

"Is Melody okay?"

"Yes. She was in a different room and trapped in the debris. Fortunately, she wasn't hit in the head, although she did break her hip and leg in several places."

"I'd like to see her," I say.

Denver smiles. "She'd love that. She's visited a few times, but you probably don't remember that."

"I'm sorry, I wish I could tell you I heard your voices, and maybe I did, but I can't recall it."

"It's okay," he assures me, and my eyelids become heavy. "Why don't you rest? You've already been through a lot."

I'm unable to fight the sleep trying to pull me under, but at least this time, when I close my eyes, it won't be for eight weeks.

Chapter Twenty-Eight

FORD

AFTER WAKING UP, I was monitored for a few days and sent to a rehabilitation center, where I would be for a while.

It's a wonderful place, but I can't wait to go home. The room is quiet right now, and I'm not sure how I feel about it.

Since I woke, life has been insane. I haven't had a moment to myself except when I'm sleeping. I'm only alone right now because I'm waiting on a visitor, and Denver had to run a few errands. His mom would normally be here with Sammy, but she wanted to give me some alone time with Melody when she arrives.

As if thinking about Melody has summoned her, I look up to see her smiling face. "Knock, knock," she calls out as she enters the room in a wheelchair.

"Hey, beautiful, lovely cast you're rocking there."

She shakes her head as she wheels herself to my bedside. "I can't wait to get this itchy thing off."

"One of the perks of being in a coma while healing is not having to deal with things like that."

"Lucky bastard," she jokes, but her smile slips. "You know we are the lucky ones, right?"

Denver filled me in on what happened after the explosion and how some officers lost their lives. My stomach rolls again at the thought.

"Do you have any insights on what happened to Brandon?"

She lets out a dry laugh. "Asshole got the easy way out. He's dead."

I'm not sure how I should respond to the news. On the one hand, I'm happy he won't be able to terrorize anyone anymore, but on the other, Melody is right. Brandon got out easy. He should have to suffer in prison. Even bad guys don't like fuckers who touch kids.

What happens now?

"I've been asking myself the same question," Melody responds, and I realize I spoke that out loud.

"I don't know if I want to go back," I tell her for the first time, even though I've been thinking about this for a while. "I've been thinking about a change for some time. I think this whole situation has solidified it for me. I want to spend more time with Sammy, and I don't want my family to constantly worry if I'll make it home each evening."

Melody presses her lips together, and a look of understanding crosses her face. "I've honestly been thinking the same. This case has been taking a toll on me. I know this is the line of work we signed up for, but Donny and I have been talking about having another kid. After everything that happened, it's just put a lot of things into perspective for me, and I want to put my family first for once."

I smile at her brightly, knowing how amazing of a mother she is. "What changed your mind? I thought you were happy with just the one."

She giggles. "I *was*... but then you had Sammy, and I got baby fever again."

I chuckle along with her. "I've heard of that happening to people. Do you have any idea what you'd want to do? I can't think of anything."

"Actually, I was toying with something but didn't want to do it alone. Now that I know you want a change of pace too, this could be perfect for us."

I raise a brow, waiting for her to continue. I'm intrigued by her excitement.

"What do you think about opening a gym?" she asks, and I almost laugh. "I know there are already so many gyms, but we would be able to offer our expertise in things like self-defense, and I know how much you loved to work out before Sammy came along," she teases.

She isn't wrong. Melody and I used to spend a lot of time in the gym together before my son was born. Denver would even join us when his schedule allowed. It's something we all enjoyed. With a few courses, we could easily become personal trainers.

"I think it's going to be a while before either of us can be personal trainers, but it gives us lots of time to do our research," I tell her.

The way her face lights up fills me with joy. "So, you're in?"

"Yeah, let's do this."

We spend some more time catching up, and after a while, there's another knock at the door.

"Am I interrupting?" Denver asks.

Melody and I shake our heads.

"I was actually just about to leave," Melody says with a warm smile. "I'll keep working on our plan. Hopefully, I can find a good location," she tells me before rolling away.

"What was that about?" Denver asks.

I can't keep the giant smile from my face. "Melody found the perfect career direction for us."

"And that would be?" he inquires, pulling up a chair next to my bed.

"We're going to open a gym. We want to focus mainly on self-defense but will obviously have a fully functioning gym for those who just want to work out. We'll probably offer other classes as well, but you know our hearts will always want to keep people safe. This is a way we can do that without having to be in the direct line of duty."

Denver's expression tells me he approves of our dream. "That's an excellent decision, but remember, you also have to focus on recovering first." His voice is firm, but his eyes are kind.

"I know, baby. It's not like we can get everything set up overnight anyway. We have a lot of things we have to plan out and get in order. But we can do that while we get our bodies back into shape."

He leans over to kiss me. "This is so you. I kind of hate that we didn't come up with this idea on our own."

I laugh. "Same, but Melody has always been the one who thinks outside the box."

"How have you been feeling today?" Denver asks.

"Honestly? I wish I could just blink and be better already."

He squeezes my hand. "I know. The process of getting you home won't be an easy one, but we can do this," he assures me.

"I can be patient and work hard if it means I get to come home to you and our boy."

He kisses me again, this time lingering on my lips. "We'll be waiting, baby. I'll also be by your side every step of the way."

The way he's staring so lovingly into my eyes assures me he's telling the truth.

"I love you," I whisper.

Denver's eyes turn glassy at my words, and he takes a ragged breath. "I love you too, and I'm so fucking happy you didn't die," he says, then gives me a few quick kisses.

I can't help but chuckle. "I'm happy I didn't die too."

My phone vibrates on the table beside the bed, and I wonder who's checking in now.

After Denver hands it to me, I stare at the screen, a little confused.

"Who is it?" he asks, and I turn the phone toward him. Denver bites his lip. "You should read it."

"Do you know something I don't know?" I ask, but he doesn't respond, so I open the message.

Mary: *Hi, Ford. Sorry for waiting so long to reach out. Samantha told me about the incident, and I wanted to make sure you were in a better place before texting.*

After you told me about your new relationship, I wasn't sure how to feel. I'm sorry for how abruptly I left. After talking with Samantha, I realized I should have handled things differently, but I also came to the realization that I needed a little help. I didn't want to contact you until I was in a better head space and got the help I needed. I feel like I'm finally in a better place, and I was hoping we could talk again.

I completely understand if you don't want to mend the bridge, but if you'll have me, I would love to be in your, Sammy's, and Denver's life.

"What do you think?" I ask Denver after I've read the message out loud.

"Honestly? I think we should give her a call. We can sit down with her and see if she's really changed. If she hasn't, then we'll say goodbye, but people deserve second chances."

"I agree."

I send a quick text asking Mary when she's available to meet. Once we've come up with a plan, I press my lips together.

"I guess we're doing this," I murmur.

"After all you've been through... this is going to be a walk in the park," Denver says with an easy smile.

I can't help but feel a little bit more at ease.

"SHE'S GOT FIFTEEN MINUTES before she said she'd be here," Denver reminds me, watching me nervously fidget with the blanket as I check the clock to see what time it is.

Again.

I roll my eyes. "I know I shouldn't be nervous, but my stomach won't stop rolling."

Denver sighs and grabs my hand, giving it a gentle squeeze. "It's going to be all right," he assures me.

"Anyone home?" a familiar voice calls out, but it isn't the one I was expecting.

"Samantha?" I gasp as she rushes to my side.

"Hey, I would have come sooner, but life has been crazy. When Mom told me she was visiting, I decided it was time to make a visit work."

That's when I notice Mary standing behind her daughter.

"Have a seat," Denver encourages them. "I don't mind standing for a little bit." He moves to the head of my bed, which has been put into a sitting position for the time being.

"I'm sorry for running out on you two when you told me you were a couple," Mary starts, taking a seat on my right. "After speaking with a therapist, I realized I had things I needed to work through. I had this false belief that Ford and Samantha would be getting back together. When you told me the two of you were dating, everything felt like it was being shaken up. I know now that neither Ford nor Samantha wanted to get back together, and that's something *I* wanted. Getting over that was a challenge, but I'm working on being a better listener and not pushing my agenda on others. I really don't have a problem that you're bi, but I can understand how I came across as homophobic. I should have just been happy that you were happy, but I was being selfish, and for that, I'm truly sorry."

"We appreciate your apology, and we are happy," I tell her, shooting a grin at Denver, whose smile matches mine.

"I really do want to be in your lives. I promise I'll keep seeing my therapist. I don't want to be a negative person, and I don't want to cause pain for anyone," she says.

Even though her reaction last time hurt, it's impossible for me to stay mad at her. "We'd love to have you in our lives, and I know Sammy would love to have his grandma back," I say.

Tears trickle down Mary's face. "Thank you," she whispers, standing to hug me.

"People make mistakes, but I'm glad to hear you're willing to put in the work to change."

She steps back, wipes her face, and sits down again. "Now, tell us more about what happened."

I tell the story I've told a few times now, and Mary and Samantha have shocked expressions on their faces as I explain the chaos of the last couple of months. Once they get over the initial upset, we fall into an easy conversation about life.

When they leave, I'm more than a little exhausted, something I've been told is normal and will get better as time goes on. It's crazy that simply having a long talk can drain me.

"Why don't you nap before your physical therapy appointment?" Denver suggests.

"Good idea," I say, pressing the button to lay the bed down. Denver kisses my head when I'm comfortable, and my eyes drift shut.

The journey to going home isn't going to be short, but at least I know the people who mean the most to me will be there whenever I finally get discharged.

Chapter Twenty-Nine

DENVER

After two months at the rehabilitation center, Ford was finally able to come home, seeing as he had the strength to move in and out of his wheelchair and do basic tasks on his own.

He's been home for about a month, and we've fallen into a comfortable routine. Thankfully, Nixon has allowed me to stay on desk duty, so while I'm still currently working, I don't have to be out in the field yet, and it allows for a lot of flexibility, which is needed with the number of appointments Ford has.

Today, Melody and I are going to be surprising Ford with a location for the gym. It's prime real estate, and when Melody brought me the listing, I knew we had to snap it up. She also agreed that surprising Ford would be perfect. The location is bare bones and is going to take a *lot* of work, but we have the time.

Ford still has months of physical therapy ahead of him before he'll even be walking on his own.

"Where are we going?" Ford asks as I help him into the car.

I shrug with a smirk. "You'll see," I reply, then close the door. "Ready for an adventure?" I ask Sammy once I'm behind the wheel.

He blows some bubbles in response and bats at the toys hanging from the handle of his car seat.

"I think that's a yes," my mom says, sitting beside him.

I chuckle as I put the car into drive and head for our destination.

"Are you really not going to tell me where we're going?" Ford asks.

I shake my head. "I thought you liked surprises," I tease.

"I like giving surprises, not so much receiving them," he mutters.

I laugh and reach over to place my hand on his shoulder. "I promise you're going to love this one."

"You're really not going to help me out on this one?" Ford asks my mom, who mimes zipping her lips.

He grumbles something under his breath, but my smile doesn't fade. I've actually got a few surprises up my sleeve for tonight, and I can't wait.

My body is humming with energy as I find a place to park and get out to help Ford get situated in his wheelchair. Mom already has Sammy in his stroller, and when I lean down to kiss his little head, he blows more bubbles at me, making my smile grow even wider.

It's still crazy to me that he is now just over six months old.

"Fancy running into you here," Melody calls out as she walks over to us.

She's still using a cane, but it's obvious her leg is getting stronger every day.

"Okay, now someone *has* to tell me what's going on," Ford complains, but none of us say anything right away.

"I'll tell you more once we get inside," Melody responds, unlocking our building.

"What is this place?" Ford asks as I push him inside.

"It's our gym," I tell him.

His eyes go wide. "Wh-what?"

"Surprise," Melody shouts.

Ford's face is pale at first, but slowly, a smile spreads across his lips. "How did you two pull this off?"

"With our combined savings and work history, we were able to get a loan at the bank," Melody supplies. "We both decided we wanted to surprise you as soon as we got the keys."

"Well, this sure is a surprise, but why did you use *your* savings?" Ford asks me, and it's time for surprise number two.

"That was something else I wanted to tell you today... I'm going to quit Hunter Security and join the two of you here... if that's okay with you?"

I wait for Ford's response with bated breath. When he beams at me, the weight resting on my chest lifts.

"It's more than okay with me. I'm so excited we're doing this," he says.

I lean down to kiss him. "There's one more thing I wanted to ask you," I whisper against his lips as I fall to one knee in front of him.

Ford gasps as I slip a box out of my back pocket.

"You've been my best friend since we were kids. I've never wanted to picture a life without you. I never expected us to end up in a relationship, but nothing in this world has ever felt more right than being a family with you and Sammy. I want us to be together forever, and I want to be able to call you my husband. Will you marry me?"

Ford nods eagerly with tears in his eyes. "Y-yes," he gasps out, and I slide the ring onto his finger.

"This is too special," Mom says as she wipes at her tears. "I can't wait to be able to call you my son, even though I've felt like your mom for a long time already."

Ford chuckles, and I use my thumb to wipe his tears away.

"I was actually wanting to ask you something too. I guess now is the perfect time," he says, and I lift my brow for him to continue. "How would you feel about adopting Sammy? I'd love for you to be listed as his father as well. I keep thinking about what would have happened had I passed away in the explosion. I don't want there to be any doubt about who Sammy goes to."

I smile and kiss him. "There is nothing I would love more."

The past six months have been a whirlwind of emotions and new experiences.

I can't wait to spend the rest of my life with my best friend and our son.

Epilogue

FORD

One year later

TODAY IS OUR GYM'S grand opening, and while we had a few setbacks that prevented us from opening as soon as we wanted, I'm glad to be standing next to my friend and my fiancé as we welcome our first customers.

"Is the self-defense class still happening this weekend?" a familiar face asks with a bright smile.

"You bet, Emelia," Denver tells her. "I'm excited for you to join us."

"Do you have lots of people signed up?" she asks.

"Yep," I say with a giant grin. "Thanks to you sharing about it on your social media account, we are booked all month."

She claps her hands and lets out a little squeal. "I'm so glad I could help. You did so much for me, both of you. I'm lucky to be alive because of you two."

There was evidence on Brandon's computer that he was planning on kidnapping Emelia eventually. He was just waiting until he had six other girls under his belt. Seven was Emelia's favorite number.

"Me too," a bright blonde with a warm smile chimes in.

"Vanessa," I call out and rush toward her, wrapping her in a hug. "You look amazing. How have you been doing?"

One of the best things that happened the day of the explosion was that Melody found Vanessa, and even though they were trapped in the debris, they both made it out alive.

"Are you coming to the self-defense class as well?" I ask her.

"Yes, and so are Cynthia and all of the girls from the club. We both realize how important it is to be able to take care of ourselves now. If I had had some basic training before, Brandon would never have been able to get me into his car. Or at least someone might have seen me fighting and called for help."

I give her another squeeze while shaking my head. "Honey, don't blame yourself."

"I know. I'm still working on that in therapy," she says.

I smile. "I'm glad you're sticking with it. I know it's helped me a lot."

"My therapist is amazing. I don't think I'll ever want to let her go," she supplies.

I chuckle. "That's amazing to hear."

After the girls leave, I go around the small party we are holding for the grand opening to talk to our friends and a few new faces excited about the gym.

The event goes by so fast, and before I know it, we're saying good-bye to everyone, and Denver and I are heading home.

"I had an idea for tonight for a special celebration," I tell Denver on the drive to our house.

He looks at me and quirks a brow. "What would that be?"

"I want you inside me tonight," I reply.

I'm glad I'm driving because I bet Denver would have driven us off the road at that suggestion.

"Are... are you serious?" he stammers.

I nod as I make a turn toward our neighborhood. "Serious as a heart attack," I tell him with a wink.

We've been discussing Denver topping me for a while, but even though it's been a long time since I've gotten the doctor's approval for sex, he's still been handling me with kid gloves. I'm ready for more and can't wait to feel my fiancé inside me. We've been using fingers, dildos, and his tongue, but it's not enough.

"Are you sure you're not tired?" he asks, bringing a smile to my lips.

To some, it might seem like he's being too cautious, but I know he truly cares about me. And I might have been known for pushing it a little too far from time to time.

"It was a long day, but I promise I'm more than ready to try this."

I cast a glance at Sammy through the rearview mirror and chuckle as a yawn escapes his mouth. I'm so glad we installed the tiny mirror on the headrest so I can see his face while I'm driving.

"Looks like Little Man is ready for bed too," I point out.

He's finally outgrown his acid reflux and is an excellent sleeper. Once he's down, we won't be interrupted until morning.

"You know all the right things to say," Denver teases with a waggle of his brows.

I wink at him because it's funny what parents find sexy. A surefire way to get into any parent's pants is to clean the kitchen and put the kid down by yourself.

Once I've pulled into the driveway, I get out and scoop Sammy out of his seat. He's almost asleep, and I decide to forgo a bath for the night. It's not like he got that dirty today.

Carefully, I carry my sleepy boy into the house and get him ready for bed. After he's in bed, I kiss his forehead and quietly shut the door on the way out.

Entering our bedroom, I'm stopped in my tracks.

"You lit candles," I whisper, stating the obvious.

"Who says I can't be romantic?" he teases.

I take long strides toward him until the gap between us is gone. As soon as he's close enough, I grab him firmly by the waist and pull him toward me, smashing my lips to his for a searing kiss.

"I love you so fucking much," I tell him when I pause for air.

"I can't wait until you're my husband," he replies, kissing me again and moving me toward the bed. "I also can't wait to get inside that virgin ass."

I chuckle as he pushes me down, then his mouth claims mine again.

We make out as we fumble to get our clothes off. I love that even though we've been together for over a year, we still can't get enough of each other. And I hope that lasts forever.

Once we're naked, Denver grabs my hand and pulls me away from the bed.

I must make a face because he laughs. "I want to shower with you first. I'm dying to eat your ass but figured we could both use a quick rinse," he states, and I stop fighting him.

We share a few passionate kisses as the water warms, then step beneath the steam spray.

Although I'm desperate to get fucked, I also love the closeness and sensuality of our showers, so I don't rush it. First, I wash Denver, paying lots of attention to his cock until my hand gets slapped.

"Do you want me to blow in here?" he grumbles.

I smirk and let him go. "You're right. I don't want to waste your load. It would be much better suited leaking out of my ass," I tease as I stand.

Denver groans as he steals the loofah from me and washes my body.

"You're so fucking perfect," he whispers as he snakes his arm around me and scrubs my crack.

His lips are once again on mine, and I moan as he thrusts his hips into me, our rock-hard cocks rubbing against each other. Our tongues dance together as we grind under the hot water. I only cut us off when it becomes hard to hold my orgasm in anymore.

"Bed. Now," I command before rinsing off and stepping out to grab us towels.

"So demanding," Denver teases.

I shake my head. "You love it."

He laughs and pecks my lips. "I do. Now come on, more fun is to be had in bed."

After we dry off, I follow him to the room and remember the candles he lit for us.

"We probably shouldn't have left those unattended," I state.

Denver nods. "Well, at least we didn't burn the house down. Now lie down so I can make you feel good," he instructs.

I do as I'm told because, even though I'm normally the one who takes the lead in the bedroom, it's still hot as fuck to give up that control from time to time. The look in my man's eyes turns me on more than I ever thought possible.

As soon as I'm lying down, Denver is between my thighs, pushing my knees up to gain access to my pucker. With speed that almost seems superhuman, he leans down and takes a nice, slow lick of an area only he's had the privilege of touching.

I throw my head back with a groan. Denver's snicker is loud in the otherwise quiet room.

"I love it when you're loud," he tells me, then gets back to work rimming my hole.

I swear my eyes damn near roll into the back of my head when he breaches me, and I cry out. I was unaware of how addicting it could be to have a tongue in your ass until the first time Denver rimmed me.

"Yes... yes... *yes*," I yell, grabbing the pillow and covering my face.

Sammy might be a fantastic sleeper, but if I'm too loud, there is a strong chance I'll wake him. And I don't need to be cockblocked right now. Not when I'm finally going to get what I've wanted for a long time.

Denver chuckles, and I hate that he's stopped. "Pass me the lube," he requests, and I begrudgingly move to grab it from the nightstand.

Thankfully, as soon as he has it in hand, he squeezes it onto his fingers, and before I know it, his thick index finger is pressing at my entrance.

"Fuck..." I hiss out as he pushes inside me.

"You like that, baby?" he asks.

I nod enthusiastically. "Want... more," I whimper out.

An evil smirk spreads across Denver's face, and he shrugs. "What if I want to take my time and tease you?" he asks as he twists his hand and rubs my prostate.

"Shit!" I gasp, my back bowing off the bed.

"You look so hot when you lose control," he states as he pushes his single finger in and out of my ass.

"Please," I beg, needing more.

"Mmm... I guess I can give you what you want."

Finally, a second finger joins the first, and he gets to work stretching me out.

Denver is a lot thicker than I am, and I know I'm going to need a lot of prep. As much as I want him to bury himself inside me now, I will need to work up to four fingers before he does that.

"More," I cry out after he's taken his sweet ass time, scissoring his two fingers and occasionally a firm milking stroke against my prostate.

Denver chuckles but *finally* adds a third finger. The intrusion of the newest digit burns, but I breathe through it, allowing my body to get used to the stretch. This time, Denver doesn't tease. He works his three fingers back and forth until I can take them to the base. Pulling them back to the tips, he adds his fourth finger, working into me and getting me good and ready for his perfect dick.

When I am good with all four digits, I feel him slow and pull them all the way out, drawing a whimper from me.

"Don't worry, babe, we aren't done yet," he assures me as he pours some lube onto his hard cock.

"Hurry," I plead.

"Ready?" he asks as he lines himself up.

I nod. "Please, baby... I need you."

Finally, he starts to push in, and the pressure is a lot, but it's also delicious.

Denver gets the head of his cock in, then waits, allowing my body time to adjust to his massive dick. He stretches me so fucking wide, but holy shit, it feels so good. Going slowly, he pushes in, widening me more and more over the increasing girth of his shaft.

"Oh God... oh God... you're so big," I pant out between gulps of air.

"Mmm... so good. You are right at the thickest part of me. I need to stretch you here so you'll be able to take each thrust. Don't worry. The rest of my shaft will slide in easily."

I'm lying spread out, legs wide open, and impaled on my man's cock. It hits me that I've never been so vulnerable before. I have never given up control so completely and utterly. I can only ever imagine having this with Denver.

As if he can feel it and hear my thoughts, he takes his big hands, runs them down my inner thighs, and circles them back out and up to my knees. He repeats the movements, soothing and relaxing me around him. I'm lulled by his hands and penetrating eyes.

"I've got you" is all he says, and it's all he needs to say. I give him my nod, and he thrusts himself the rest of the way inside me.

His balls smack against my ass, and I'm filled, full of him. My head spins for a split second as the pleasure radiates through me.

Grabbing my legs, he wraps them around his waist and leans in to kiss me.

"You... feel... so good," I tell him between pants.

He smiles against my lips. "Now you know what it's like," he replies.

When he kisses me again, I lick the seam of his lips, sighing when he opens and letting our tongues dance together. I love our connection and can feel how we pour our love into each other through our kisses.

I've grown desperate for more and am ready for him to move.

"Please, I need more. I need you to take me and fuck me... I want you to claim me as yours," I whisper.

Denver smiles at me and gently rocks his hips, giving me a few shallow easy thrusts.

My body lights up as this euphoria washes over me. I thought fucking Denver was the best thing in the world, but this is something else entirely.

"So... good, I didn't know it would feel... so... fucking... good," I moan as he fucks me with such care, but I want more. "More... *please*," I beg.

"Are you sure?" Denver asks.

"Please. Fuck me hard. Give me everything. I want it all. I need you."

Denver kisses me again and hammers his hips into mine, swallowing all my cries of pleasure.

I had no idea being fucked by the man I love would feel like this. It's so good, but it's more than sex. It's the connection we share as we make love.

Denver does what I ask. He doesn't hold back. He maneuvers one of my legs over his body in an unexpected move between thrusts and rolls me on my side. Continuing to pound into me, he grabs onto my hip and pulls, and together, we have me on all fours.

Grabbing onto my shoulder at the base of my neck, he pulls me into him with each thrust of his shaft. I thought the other position was amazing, but this one has his shaft grazing my prostate.

We work our bodies together, and we're dripping with sweat before long. Denver's thrusts are getting harder, and the rhythm is choppier. He's close, but for me, the need to come is there, almost as if I can't reach the climax. It's so close yet so far away.

As if reading my body, Denver pulls on my shoulder, pulling me up so my back is to his chest. This changes everything. Now, instead of just grazing my prostate, his cock presses more firmly into it with each thrust.

Moaning, my head falls back onto his shoulder in ecstasy. His strong arms wrap around me, one across my chest and shoulders, the other low over my hip and down to my weeping and hard dick.

He holds me tight to the solidness of his body. I'm entirely caught up in him, thoroughly ensnared, and I can only take what he gives me. I take the pounding of his cock into my willing body and lose myself in the pleasure of his hand roughly stroking my cock, accepting the control he has over me right now.

"You feel so good here in my arms, my whole length being taken into your tight hole. But I want to feel you come on my cock. Are you going to come for me?" he asks me with a ragged breath.

"Yes," I whisper.

"Good, come for me, baby," he commands, then turns my head and slams his mouth into mine. That's all I needed. I let go, and my roar is swallowed up by his eager mouth. My cum coats his hand as he pumps me dry.

"Fuck," Denver yells into my mouth, spilling his load into my ass. The warmth fills me up, and it's so hot.

After a few more thrusts, milking himself dry, my man stops shaking and collapses into me. We fall forward to the bed, catching ourselves partially, and flop together on our sides.

"That was perfect," I whisper.

"Mmm... so good. But if I had to choose one, I still think I prefer bottoming," he adds while pulling out.

I chuckle, turning to face him. "Good thing we don't have to choose, then. We can do it both ways."

For a while, I hold my sexy fiancé before we decide it's time to clean up. Then, on deadened legs, we make our way to the bathroom.

Once our bodies are free of cum, we climb back into bed and snuggle up.

This is exactly how I love to spend each night, and I'm so happy I'll be able to do that for the rest of my life.

I always knew I wanted Denver in my life forever, and I'm so fucking happy we figured out that it was better to be more than friends.

THE END

I really hope you enjoyed Ford and Denver! If you did please leave an honest review!

Don't want to say goodbye to Ford, Denver and Sammy just yet? Download the bonus epilogue here! (Sammy is a very comical toddler at his Dads wedding)

Up next is **Knox: A Suspenseful M/M Brother's Best Friend Romance** coming to Amazon and Kindle Unlimited Nov 16, 2023! Pre-Order Today.

Also By Laura John

*** Indicates M/M romance

Love In Sienna Series

1. Secret Smiles (A friends to lovers rock star romance) *ALSO AVAILABLE IN AUDIO!*

2. Hidden Kisses (An enemies to lovers baseball romance)

3. Guarded Hearts (A New adult, best friends to lovers, single mother romance.

4. Whispered Desires (A single mother, enemies to lovers, age gap, rock star romance)

5. **Confidential Moments (A M/M Baseball romance)*****

6. Clean Slates (A fast burn rock star romance)

7. Tangled Love (A rock star romance love triangle romance)

8. Restless Beat (A rock star romance)

9. Love In Sienna Boxset (Books 1-4)

10. Love in Sienna Boxset (Books 5-8)

Sentinel Protection Duology

1. **Fighting Attraction (A M/M bodyguard romance)*****

2. **Embracing Temptation (A M/M age gap bodyguard romance)*****

Standalones

1. Monster In The Shadows (Dark romance standalone)

2. **Kissing in the snow (A M/M Christmas Novella set in the Sentinel Protection World)*****

3. Afterglow (A kinky brother's best friend romance)

Acknowledgements

WHERE DO I START? There are always so many people to thank and this book is no different.

First, I'd like to say fuck you to the Alberta Fires of 2023 as they completely derailed me and took a major toll on my mental health. But of course, I refused to let them hold me back.

I should probably start by thank you's with my amazing team. Brittany Franks and Suzanne Talkington are the reason I didn't break down completely. They were a listening ear and a kick in the pants when needed. I don't know where I'd be without these two amazing women. They are seriously my ride-or-dies and I am so thankful to have them in my life.

And while I'm talking about Brittany Franks... she needs a second shout-out for creating the AMAZING cover! I am always so blown away with how talented she is!

Next to my amazing alpha/beta readers. Robin, Mandy, and Shannon are an absolute blast to work with and really help me nail down the first and second drafts of my books. They are also an amazing sounding board when I hit a wall and need to figure out where I'm going. I am never letting these ladies go.

My FANTASTIC sensitivity reader JP. This man is the only reason I feel confident writing M/M romance. I know that he will tell me if I get things wrong (he's done it before). I love how outspoken and unapologetically himself he is. I am more than happy to be able to call JP my friend!

My editing team who are the real MVPs this time around. Let's just say that thanks to the forest fires this book was a little bit rougher than I would have liked... But that didn't stop my editing team from helping me polish this book into the amazing version it is today! So a big shout out to Chantell, Kay, Nadara, and Nikki with Swish Design and Editing

My husbands for being understanding when I had to hunker down in my writing cave and the house fell apart. I couldn't continue to be on this writing journey without his love and support. He will forever be my rock and the one I turn to for everything. He means the world to me and I'm so lucky to have in my life.

During the writing of Denver, I asked my readers group to come up with some stripper names and they did not disappoint! Thank you to Mandy Williams for the name petal and Michelle Lynn Bragg for the name Trixie!

And last but not least, thank YOU! If you weren't reading my books, I wouldn't continue to do this!

About Author

LAURA IS A STEAMY romance author from Alberta, Canada, who melds love and angst together while normalizing mental illness. She also brings a mixture of m/m and m/f books because love is love. In her books, you will fall in love with her rock stars, bodyguards, baseball players, a small town and even a hired hit man!

When she's not writing, Laura enjoys reading, going to concerts, hiking, and experimenting with makeup!

You can find Laura online here:

Made in the USA
Middletown, DE
13 October 2023